De_____yers

by Dave & Cherry McKay

copyright 2008

Published by
Friends Learning Resources
P.O. Box 8648,
Nairobi, 00200,
Kenya

Email: friendslearningresources@gmail.com

ISBN: 9966-755-42-X

Printed by Print Shop Pvt. Ltd.
Chennai, India

About the Book

"Destroyers" is the third book in a trilogy by Dave McKay, all covering the same period in earth's history, at a time when disasters threaten to destroy the entire planet.

This book looks at events from the perspective of a poor, handicapped young man living in a remote village in Kenya. Moses Chikati struggles to make a living for himself and his sister by carrying passengers on his bicycle from place to place on the dirt roads of the Kenyan interior.

For Moses, the major events of the world are of little consequence except as they relate to his daily needs; but in the process of trying to get ahead he finds himself travelling the world and even playing a key role in events that shape history.

Will success bring him happiness? Or will it destroy him?

There is something of Moses Chikati in each of us.

Page Listings

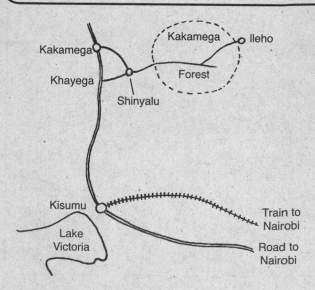

Introduction--Shinyalu

Shinyalu was not so different from any one of a thousand other villages in Western Kenya. It was a collection of small shops (mostly butchers with chopping blocks for counters and fly-covered meat hanging beside the blocks) and open-air stalls selling produce, used clothing, pots, tools, and hand-made goods out of handcarts or just from tarps spread on the ground. The village had a post office, general store, hardware shop, *kinyosi**, and numerous cafes which served up generous portions of *ugali**, beans, and *sukuma wiki**. On market days Shinyalu would attract a thousand or more shoppers, coming to sell their livestock and/or to stock up on essentials.

Shinyalu was situated at the T-junction of two dirt roads, one going east to the Kakamega Forest (and west to the paved road that leads south to Kisumu, on the shores of Lake Victoria); and the other going north to Kakamega, where locals could get most of their "luxury" items: furniture, windows, anything electrical, and exotic foods like pineapples, potatoes, or chocolate.

Smack in the middle of the T-junction there were always *matatus** and at least half a dozen *boda-boda** drivers parked, waiting for business. Vehicles actually negotiating the road would simply drive around them, being careful not to move too close to the edges, where the camber was so steep that they were constantly in danger of slipping into deep rainwater drains that extended down both sides of the road.

Swahili definitions appear in a list on page 188.

Roads like these linked villages throughout the interior. In the dry season they were a series of rock-hard ruts and pot holes, that threatened the suspensions of anything that dared to travel on them. In the wet, they turned into slippery ooze that regularly sucked vehicles into the drains, where driver and passengers would be forced to wait for sufficient volunteers to drag them out, using strong ropes wrapped around the nearest tree.

A hundred metres east of the markets, on the road to Kakamega, lived Amy Walker. Amy was a thin, softly spoken, unmarried Australian Aborigine, in her late fifties. Amy had a twitch in her left eye, which had led to her being called Winky by those who knew her well. She had been raised by a European family in North Queensland, but fifteen years earlier she had become convinced that she should go and live with her "people". Amy believed that the Australian Aborigines had, centuries ago, migrated there from Kenya, and that the way to find her spiritual roots would be to return to Africa. Here in this remote corner of Kenya, she had learned to speak fluent Swahili, as well as Luhya, the more popular local dialect. Over the years, people in the village had ceased to think of her as an Australian, and had come to accept her as one of their own. One by one, she took in selected orphans, until she had nine additions to her household.

An independent Pentecostal church in Queensland had sponsored Amy at the start, but two years after she left Australia, she had a falling out with them over religious differences. Amy had been forced to find support from other sources ever since. Although she had been granted Kenyan citizenship, the local government offered her no help with finances. Nevertheless, circumstances and her own doggedness had led Amy to enough individual supporters over the years to provide her with a dilapidated van and a four-room brick building to house her and the children who lived with her.

The house had no running water or electricity, but it and the van were considered luxuries by her less fortunate neighbours. Locals often used those luxuries to argue that Amy owed it to them to take on more of the workload in caring for hundreds of orphans in the area.

"You can only scratch as far as your arm can reach," she would reply, quoting a local proverb. "If I try to do too much, we all lose."

Nevertheless, she was often pressed into assisting in other ways, as readers will soon see.

The most notable thing about Shinyalu, about Amy, and about all of the people living in Shinyalu, was just how typically unnotable they were. There are thousands of similar villages throughout the world, all populated by the poorer half of the planet's citizens. People in them live and die without anyone from the major metropolises ever knowing a thing about them. Entire villages could be wiped out, through disease, famine, civil war, natural disasters, or political genocide, and the rest of the globe -- those who think they know what is really happening in the world today -- might never even hear of it.

But this is the story of one singularly unnotable *boda-boda* driver, from that one unnotable village, who came to be part of events that shaped the world.

Chapter 1--Trouble

"Please, Madam, I have a trouble... *please.*"

It was very late on a Friday night in January. An unseasonal light rain was falling. Amy Walker had sent Benjamin to the door in response to a weak knock.

"Open it, Benjie," she said when Benjamin hesitated at opening to a stranger so late at night. Amy was fully occupied holding Karla, the youngest of nine orphans who lived with her. Benjie, at 18, was the oldest, and he had awakened her when the baby started vomitting.

Light from the lantern on the floor was visible from the road. It was the only light still showing on that side of the village.

"Wah! What happened?" Benjie exclaimed in shock as he opened the door.

The young boy slumped into Benjie's arms before he could answer.

"Winky, it's Moses Chikati! He's bleeding! Real bad!" Benjie struggled to hold the boy up and deal with the blood at the same time. Moses Chikati, the 14-year-old son of a local butcher, had been tightly holding his right bicep prior to the collapse, but when he let go, blood poured from below the elbow of his badly cut forearm.

Amy laid Karla on the floor and rushed to Benjie's aid. What she saw would have been too much for most people, but not her. The lad's forearm had been badly broken, just below the elbow. It had been sliced halfway through, causing it to dangle as though separated. Fortunately the main arteries did not appear to have been severed.

"Lay him here, and wake Anna, eh," Amy told Benjie. At 16, Anna was the second oldest of the orphans.

Amy elevated the injured arm, to minimise blood flow, and squeezed hard just above his elbow. It took both her hands to do it, one encircling the skinny bicep, and the other struggling to keep the half-severed piece in line with the rest of the arm.

When Benjie returned with Anna, they used an old rag to make a tourniquet, which Amy applied, before resting the entire arm on the boy's stomach and carrying him to Amy's old Hi-Ace. Benjie climbed in first and then helped pull Moses in after him. He had to kneel over the lanky body that lay in the aisle between the seats.

Anna stayed to clean up the blood and care for the children, while Amy and Benjie headed for the hospital. Amy had thought of taking Karla too, but knew it was just a matter of time before the baby's fever would break, and this was far more urgent.

In the wet, slippery conditions, she had to struggle to keep the vehicle from sliding off either side of the road on the ten kilometre trip to Kakamega. They reached the hospital in half an hour, a good time in the wet, especially at night.

Moses was still breathing, but his heartbeat was weak as they carried him into the hospital. The night nurse called for the doctor, and Amy, who was type O, donated blood, which was given to him while they waited. When the medico arrived, he assured her that Moses would be fine. Amy and Benjie then left for the journey home.

Chapter 2--Assistance

The next morning the village of Shinyalu was abuzz with what had happened overnight. Fred Chikati, a local butcher, had attacked his wife with a meat cleaver in a drunken rage, and brutally killed her. Moses had been injured while trying to protect his mother, and had fled in the direction of Winky Walker's house, probably because it was the only one with a light on at that hour. His younger sister, Rosy, though uninjured, had been found cowering in a corner in shock, when neighbours went to investigate the screams.

The police had come to Amy's door shortly after she and Benjie returned from the hospital. They were, of course, looking for information, but Amy was little help, apart from telling them where she had taken Moses, and what his condition was. The sun was just coming up when the police left.

Later that morning, Fred was found sleeping in a nearby maize field and the police dragged him off to the local lock-up, where a stiff beating gave them all the information they would need to lock him away for the rest of his life.

That same afternoon, Fred Chikati's brother, George, came by with young Rosy. He wanted Amy to take the two youngsters in as orphans.

"They ain't orphans," Amy whispered angrily, hoping that Rosy would not understand if she used English. "They're your family; *you* take them." All of the kids staying with her had lost both parents to AIDS, and none of them had any other living relatives. She had refused to help literally hundreds of other orphans in the area because they did not match those criteria. Locals knew her rules, and most respected it; but George did not let that deter him.

"We'll not take them," he said. "They're cursed, Madam. A bad spirit will come on us if we help them."

"Don't be stupid," said Amy. "A bad spirit will come on you if you *don't* help them. They're your *kin*."

Her words had little effect. When George returned to the markets he left Rosy on the road in front of Amy's house, with a strong warning for her not to follow him.

"C'mon in, girl," Amy said to Rosy when George was gone. Rosy was 11, two and a half years younger than Moses, who had turned fourteen just before Christmas. Both children were big for their age.

Rosy was not talking. But she laughed... a strangely happy laugh. She used it (and a word or two here and there) to respond to Amy's questions. For all Amy knew, this was how she always communicated.

Amy was able to get information out of Rosy just by asking the right questions and by watching how she laughed in response. Through this, she learned that Rosy was afraid to return to the butcher shop; and through her own children she learned that the family had a small *shamba* nearby, with a mud hut on it. Their father had only been renting the butcher shop, and so it would no longer be available to the children now that he was in jail.

Rosy stayed at Amy's overnight, and the next day, Sunday, Amy took her out to the *shamba*, along with Lucy and the twins. Lucy was seven, and Jane and Gene were nine. The land was in the process of being prepared for planting, and the hut looked like it had been used from time to time.

"Do you sleep here?" Amy asked.

Rosy laughed in a way that expressed embarrassment, and she shook her head vigorously.

"Did Moses stay here?"

Same reaction.

"So who stayed here?"

She raised her eyebrows, laughed again, then screwed her face up in disgust. "Bad lady," was all she said.

Whoever it was, Rosy obviously did not approve.

From the hut Rosy picked up a *jembe*, a short handled heavy hoe, and she proceeded to drop it forcefully into thick grass that had grown around the edges of the tiny block, and then to lever the grass out before turning each piece of sod upside-down to die. Soon she had enticed Gene into using the hoe, while she checked on a few other things. As Amy looked on, he got the feeling that it had been Rosy's job to farm the tiny plot.

Amy also worked out from a few gestures and words that a larger, neighbouring block belonged to the children's uncharitable uncle, George Chikati.

Kenyan parents divide their land up between their sons. With each new generation, the plots become smaller. Some sons sell out to their brothers, then move to cities like Nairobi and Mombasa; but for those who stay, just surviving on what they can grow on an acre, then half an acre, and then a quarter of an acre becomes more and more impossible with each new generation. No doubt the uncle wanted to see the children disposed of, so that he could claim back his brother's share of the family plot.

On Monday, when most of the children were off at school, Amy decided to leave Benjie in charge and take another trip to the hospital in Kakamega to check on Moses. Rosy came with her.

When they were in the hallway, before entering Moses' ward, Amy detected a hurried movement in the boy's bed about the same time that the nurse cleared them to enter the room.

Moses had a big grin on his face. Rosy ran over to him and leaned her head on his left shoulder, both to comfort him and to comfort herself at the same time.

"Me, I got a surprise, Madam," Moses said, looking over Rosy's head at Amy. "Watch this, Rosy," he added, and then, with a flourish, he pulled his right arm out from under the sheet.

Amy was shocked to see that the boy's arm had been cut off, below the elbow. Moses was displaying a heavily bandaged stump. And he was treating it like a joke! His resilience was amazing; but Amy was furious.

"Wait here," was all she could say as she turned to race back out of the room.

"What have they done to him? What have they done?" she whispered to the duty nurse in something close to a shout. "They didn't need to do that."

"Madam, you need to talk to the doctor about that. We don't have specialists here for putting pins and wires in; so he just took. That was better for him."

"Easier maybe, but not *better*," Amy said in disgust, as she turned to walk back into the room. The boy's life could be ruined just because of their indifference!

Moses was busy talking to Rosy, who was still only responding with laughs and giggles. It was hard to believe they had just lost both of their parents and one arm.

"You must not go with her. We will lose the land," Moses was explaining in Luhya.

"*Sawa*," Rosy managed to say in response, before adding her signature giggle, to show support for her brother's logic.

"Thank you, Madam, for helping me," Moses said to Amy in English, when he saw her approaching the bed. "Me, I think I woulda been gone -- they said that -- if you did not assist, I would be over the mountain and gone."

Amy was witnessing what she would come to see as trademarks of the young boy. One was his command of language. He could have easily spoken to her in Luhya, but he enjoyed using English, and he would often use it in the strangest ways... not because he lacked vocabulary, but rather because he had more vocabulary than he knew what to do with.

The other trademark was his spontaneous good nature... an ability to stay positive in the face of any adversity. These were qualities that were destined to take him to the top of the world.

Chapter 3--A Loan

"Madam, we got a trouble again. Please, can you give some help?" It was early Friday morning and Moses was back at Amy's door with Rosy at his side. He had been out of hospital two days, and, with his sister, had moved into the mud hut on their land, 400 metres down the road from where Amy lived. Their mother's body had been buried on her family's property the day before, because Fred had never paid a dowry. It made matters worse for the children, who were now more or less illegitmate.

"Show her, Rosy," he said, and Rosy turned to the side while lifting her blouse to show two round burn marks on her lower back. Amy bent down to get a closer look, and reached out to gingerly touch one of the burns. Rosy drew back in pain, but still managed a laugh.

"How did this happen?" Amy asked, although she knew without asking.

"He wants the land, madam, pure and easy. He put cigarettes on her back. Even he will do it again if we sleep there. Last night we laid in a *shamba* down the road. But we need the land, Madam!"

Rosy lowered her blouse and looked up at Amy with eyes that spoke sadness, but a mouth that still smiled.

"One second and I'll come with you," Amy said. Her children had just sat down to breakfast in the crowded living room, and so Benjie was put in charge.

On the walk out to the property, Amy asked Moses how his arm was.

"It hurts where it isn't," he said in English. "Me, I can't comfort it now... because it's not there."

Rosy skipped ahead and turned to take a swing at Moses' phantom right hand. He instinctively pulled back and she laughed.

"You know English too!" Amy remarked. She had assumed that Rosy's shyness meant she was not as smart as Moses.

To reach Moses' land, the trio needed to walk down a narrow path that passed through his uncle's land. George saw them coming and was waiting.

"They are not wanted here," he said to Amy. "They will bring trouble to my family. The curse is on them."

"And the D.O. will be on to you," said Amy. She hated to use her friendship with the District Officer as a threat, because she knew that anyone with more wealth than herself might be able to make a similar threat to her if they chose to.

"I have other friends," warned George; but Amy knew he did not have any powerful enough to sway the D.O.

"And I have the burns that you gave to Rosy," Amy warned. "If you lay one more finger on her, I'll have you taken in and dealt with. True!"

Being "dealt with" was a guaranteed twenty lashes from a whip, standard interrogation in those parts; but it could also mean languishing in a cell for months, or even years, just *waiting* to be heard in court. Amy wasn't sure if she would follow through on such a threat, but George knew there would be no mercy for him if she did.

"It isn't enough land to feed them. They cannot come to me if they get hungry," he warned, which was his way of conceding defeat.

"We won't do that, Uncle," Moses promised, before pushing past him with a flourish from his good left arm, and leading the two females onto the land that was now rightfully his.

"It's true, you know," Amy reminded Moses, when they were out of earshot of George. "You won't be able to feed yourselves with what you can grow here. Have you thought about that?"

"Madam, I been designing on that already. I reckon if I had a *boda-boda*, we could manage fine."

"But how would you drive with only one arm?" Amy asked, feeling awkward about mentioning something that Moses himself seemed oblivious to. There was no answer, and so she assumed she had made him aware of something that he had not previously considered.

After an awkward silence, conversation moved to other things, and there was no further mention of the boy's plans. Moses wanted to show Amy that he could still swing the *jembe* fine with just his left arm, and he took a few swings; but Amy cautioned him about exerting too much with *either* arm before the stitches had been removed from the stump. She forced herself not to get too involved, however. She had her own family to worry about, and in the end, Moses and Rosy Chikati would need to sort out their problems by themselves. Such was life in rural Kenya.

A few Saturdays later, Amy received another knock on her door. This time it was Rosy, and she was jumping up and down with excitement.

"Come! See!" she shouted, laughing almost hysterically to make it clear that she was bringing good news.

Amy rushed to the door and saw Moses barrelling up the dirt road from the markets with a trail of dust behind him, and a passenger on the back of a *boda-boda*. He pulled up in front of Amy's house, let his passenger off and then handed the bike over to that same passenger.

"Jidraph borrows me his bike when he's having a rest. I been getting lots of practice." he said, only slightly out of breath from his exhibition ride. "Me, I just need a ten-speed, like Jiddy, and I can ride fine. Starting is the hardest, but the gears, they just help." Jiddy smiled at the compliment, before heading back toward the village.

A bike of any sort was too much for Moses to afford, and a ten-speed was considered a luxury even amongst the other *boda-boda* drivers. Jiddy was the only one in Shinyalu with one.

"Where are you going to get money for something like that?" Amy asked, knowing that he had been hoping she would help him out.

She then proceeded to share with him some of her own philosophy about money.

"My White mama always said 'Waste not, want not.' What that means is don't spend what you don't have. Then if you need it, you'll have it. You understand?"

"We're not wasting, Madam," Moses said politely. "But we're needing... real soon. Last year's maize is running to nothing, and we only just planted for this year. It'll be September before we get more."

Amy knew before the words had left her mouth that she had been preaching to herself and not to Moses when she lectured about thrift. She had seen many Kenyans get money and then waste it. The same had been true of her people in Australia. So the sermon was one that she often preached. But none of this applied to Moses. He had not done anything wrong, and he did not have anything to waste, even if he had wanted to.

The lecture had been a vain attempt to compensate for her own feelings of futility. Living within her means had always worked for her and the kids, although even now they were going through one of the leanest periods that she had ever experienced. Two of her three best supporters from Australia had stopped sending contributions. Otherwise, she might have had something to help Moses get started with herself.

There was a little micro-bank in Kakamega that she knew would loan the money for a bike, but borrowing was a sin in her books. Still, she couldn't just stand by and do nothing.

"You know, Moses, borrowing money is an awful way to live. Most people who do it, just keep borrowing more and more, and it makes them slaves to the ones they borrow from."

"Yes, Madam," Moses said, trying hard to understand what she was getting at.

"But if you were very very careful -- and I can help you with this -- maybe you could just this once borrow for a bike... a ten-speed if you like. You know, boy, if it was up to me and if I had it, I'd give you the money myself. But I just don't have it. There's a place in Kakamega where you can get a loan. You could pay them back from what you earn each week. If I took you there, would you be sure to pay them back, fast as you can?"

"Oh yeah, you bet, Madam. Hear that, Rosy? We can borrow some money to get started."

Amy cringed on hearing Moses react so enthusiastically to an offer of credit. She vowed to compensate for her sin by teaching him everything she knew about getting out of debt and staying out, so that she would not be responsible for any damage that might come from such a decision so early in his life.

The next day they went to town. With Amy's recommendation, Moses had no problem getting the loan. He ordered a ten-speed an hour later. If it had been a regular bike, he could have taken delivery then and there, but it would be a week before a ten-speed could be trucked up from Nairobi.

On the drive back to Shinyalu, Moses commented on the steep descent down to the river crossing, and the hill on the other side.

"Jiddy can just ride up with a passenger, but the others walk them up. Even me, I have to walk it. But it's the only place where I do. I been over this whole road on Jiddy's bicycle."

Rosy just grinned and giggled, with her hands clasped in her lap, kind of bouncing on the seat in anticipation of Moses starting work in a week's time.

Chapter 4--A Tight Budget

Over the next few months, Moses would stop by Amy's on the way back to his hut each night, when the kids were all in bed or close to it. With Amy's help, he would count his takings for the day, record it in a little notebook, and then put most of the money away where it would be safe. They worked out a budget that would enable him to repay the loan in half the time he had been allowed, and he was putting some aside for emergencies too... repairs, sickness, bad weather, seeds for the farm. It left him and his sister barely enough for the most basic food, but Moses loved the challenge.

"You know, my *baba* wasn't all bad, Winky," he said without warning one evening in May, when they were just locking up the little metal box that held his earnings. Amy had taught him to address her by name as all the children did. "He was real nice when he wasn't drinking," Moses went on.

He had often talked about missing his mother, but It was the first time Moses had brought up the subject of his father, and so Amy sat back in an old soft chair to listen.

"Tell me about him," she said.

"He killed Mama, I know, and that was awful," the boy said, taking a seat across the room from Amy. "*Baba* had other women, too, down at the hut. But he was always regretting. Hated himself. He told me so."

Then Moses just sat quietly for a moment, thinking, before he spoke again.

"It was you talking about money that made me reminisce of him," he said. "*Baba* talked to me like that many times... not about money, but about drinking mostly. Made me promise never to do it. He said we had good blood... kind blood, if the alcohol didn't get in it. I don't like what he did to mama; but I'm goin' ta keep my promise, Winky."

"That's good!" said Amy with deep feeling and a motherly smile. "You do that and you won't never regret it."

Business was good for Moses, and Moses was good at business. He had painted, as well as he could with his left hand, the words "Waste not; Want not" on the bike's mud flap as a reminder. He wasn't as fast as the older drivers, but there were people who would still choose him over the others when there were several waiting at the stand. Was it the thrill of riding on a ten-speed, or maybe they felt sorry for him because of his young age and his missing arm? It was hard to tell. He didn't want pity, and he would sometimes refuse a customer when other drivers had been waiting longer than himself. But he knew that, if it *was* the ten-speed attracting customers, in time, the novelty would wear off; he would need something else to bring in business.

Moses had one final piece of news to share with Amy that evening. It hadn't been mentioned earlier because he was nervous about how she would take it.

"Man from the micro-bank came to the village today," he said.

"Really?" asked Amy suspiciously. "What kind of business would he have way out here?"

"Took my picture!" said Moses with a proud grin. "For making a movie thing."

"He came all the way out here to take your picture?" Amy asked, still doing nothing to hide her suspicion.

"He wanted to see me ride the bike, and talk to people. Stuff like that. I was show acting for more than an hour. I missed a lot of fares because of it; but afterwards they all wanted to ride with me so I could tell them for myself what happened."

"And what *is* happening?" asked Amy, whose eye was twitching more than usual.

"They're making a testimonial or something, to show people how the bank works. I just talked about my testimony 'n stuff."

"Did they pay you anything?" Amy asked.

"No, but he gave a soda."

"I suppose it won't do no harm," said Amy. "But remember, son, you don't have to pose for pictures if you don't want."

"Me, I didn't do it cuz I *had* to, Amy. I did it because it was fun."

"Fair enough. Anyway, it's time for you to get on home. Rosy will be wondering what's happened."

The days were long for the two siblings, with Rosy working the *shamba* after school, and Moses putting in twelve to fourteen hours on the bike. He packed *chapatis* or *ugali* for lunch each day, but by knock-off time each evening, he was always starved. Rosy would have hot beans, *ugali*, and *sukuma wiki* waiting for him at home, and so he hurried off.

Chapter 5--Josephat

It was early June when Moses listened to Josephat for the first time in his life. He had seen him in the village a few times over the years, and had heard people talk about this strange wandering prophet, but he had never taken the time to actually listen to the man when he was younger. Josephat would just appear in a village in the morning, after having slept out in the open or on a door-step from sometime in the middle of the night. He would stay for a few days, and then disappear as he had appeared, without warning, sometime during the night. Josephat walked wherever he went over the Kenyan interior, wearing a black felt hat and a robe-like covering made of rabbit skins. In his right hand was a beautifully carved walking stick, which, like the robe, was his own creation. No one knew exactly where the hat came from, but it added to the overall look of eccentricity.

People in the village listened to Josephat politely as he sat on the steps of the post office quietly sharing his message; but they were not about to join him in his strange lifestyle.

Western Kenya was mostly divided between Catholics, Quakers, and various Pentecostal and traditional sects. The Protestants took Josephat more seriously than the Catholics, but Catholics listened too. Moses didn't go to any church, but he was intrigued by Josephat's strange dress, and by things he had heard. It was midday and one of the busiest times for *boda-boda* drivers, but Moses left the stand and wheeled his bike over closer to the crowd, so he could pick up on what was being said.

·"God's going to destroy those that destroys the earth," Josephat was saying quietly. He didn't shout like so many of the street preachers who frequented the village. He spoke quietly, and the people listened patiently, occasionally interjecting or asking a question.

"I think it's close now," he went on. "You can't trust the churches no more; the government is full-on corrupt; and the people are all sinning bad as ever. It's bad times. Won't be long till he destroys those that destroys the earth, like he sade in The Revelation."

"People been saying that for a long time, Josephat," said Obadiah, the postmaster, who had come out from behind the counter to listen; no one could get in or out of the post office anyway, not while Josephat was there. Obadiah was a respected elder in the Upendo Congregation of the Faithful, Church of the Holy Spirit, and a regular listener to Josephat's pronouncements. "I'm not saying you're wrong, brother, but I been hearing that for must be 20 years now."

"So we're 20 years closer now than we was when you first heard it," Josephat replied with a smile, and the crowd supported him, some because they could see the humour in what he was saying, and some because they could see the truth. Josephat himself had only been preaching in those parts for the past 10 or 12 years.

"We hafta be ready, brothers and sisters. We hafta be ready," he said to the crowd.

"And how do you think we can do that?" asked Obadiah.

"You hafta learn how to listen to the voice of the Spirit. Not your churches and your leaders, and not your own natural thinking. Just listen to the Spirit... honest and humble-like."

"And what if we can't hear no voices like you?" someone from the crowd interjected.

"You *can* hear," Josephat argued. "Not like I'm talking right now, you can't, but in your heart. You just have to be still enough and be real quiet in your spirit. Push away all your own thinking and your doubts, and you'll hear God talking... same as in your conscience."

"And what's he goin' ta say?" the same voice asked with a clear touch of cynicism.

"Different things to different peoples," Josephat answered, straight-faced. "But I know he'll say *ni lazima* about getting ready."

"Ready for what, Josephat?" This question, from Obadiah, was expressed more sympathetically.

"Ready for the troubles. They's going to be troubles. Worst troubles in the history of everything. I can't say what you need to do, cuz some of it's secrets, just for the dearly beloved. You hafta ask Him if you want to find out. But real soon now, he's goin' ta destroy them that's destroying the world. That's what he told me."

Moses couldn't see much difference in what Josephat was saying and what he had heard other locals say... especially the Pentecostals. Jesus coming back. End of the world. It didn't seem to make much difference in the way they lived, though. So what was the point?

Of course it did make a difference to Josephat, and that was probably why people listened so intently to him when he came through. He would turn up in the village maybe once or twice a year, sometimes carrying a plastic container of honey, or at some other time carrying bowls which he had carved from local wood. He never sold his stuff, just gave it to different people. But others gave him things that he needed too... maize mostly. It could have been how he got the felt hat that had become one more item in his overall image. He would only ever stay long enough to preach for a few days -- like he was doing now -- before moving on.

That night when Moses arrived at Amy's, she offered him some honey with his tea.

"Where'd you get that, Winky?" he asked gruffly.

"A friend gave it to me," she said with a smile.

"You mean that old preacher man with the walking stick, don't you?" Moses stated. "I didn't know he was your friend." He was definitely not impressed.

"Has been for a couple of years," Amy answered.

"So you believe the stuff he saze?"

"Depends on what stuff," answered Amy.

"End of the world stuff," said the youngster.

"I do and I don't," she answered cryptically. "It's more spiritual for me... being ready to die... doing what God wants. Stuff like that."

Something strange was happening. Moses didn't think of Amy as a mother. She had her family, and there wasn't time for her to be more than a friend to him. So he didn't feel jealous about the time she gave to the other children. But something about her having this friendship with Josephat bothered him. Why hadn't Winky ever said anything to him before, about Josephat being her friend? And what business did he have with her in the first place? A bit of honey didn't give him the right to mess with her head if, in fact, that was what he was doing.

All of this was going through Moses' mind in a way that clashed with his normally clear thinking. He could see that he was reacting strangely, but he still believed the problem lay with Josephat and not with himself. Josephat wasn't just messing with Winky's mind; he was messing with his too. And Moses didn't like it.

"Son, Josephat is doing the best he knows to serve his God, same as you trying hard to care for Rosy," Amy explained. "We each have our jobs to do, and the Good Lord has the final word on us all."

"Yeah, sure," Moses said, looking uncharacteristically glum. But not for long. He just didn't have the disposition to stay upset for long.

"Anyway, let's count the money," he said, bouncing back in that incurably optimistic way of his. "Me, I got a couple of big fares this afternoon. I wanna see if it evenates for what I missed at lunch time."

Chapter 6--An Exciting Offer

Two weeks later, in the mid-afternoon, Moses turned up just as Amy was changing Karla's nappy.

"Get the door for Amy," she said to Jo-Jo, a four-year-old who was the only one of the children other than Karla, who was not in school.

Little Jo-Jo opened the door and then just looked over his shoulder at Amy.

"Who is it?" Amy asked.

"Mo-Mo," the toddler responded.

"C'mon in, Moses!" Amy shouted.

"I have someone, Winky. Can he come in too?"

"Sure, bring him in. I'll just be a minute with Karla."

Moses came in, followed by the man from the micro-bank in Kakamega. Amy recognised him from when she had taken Moses in to get his loan.

"This is Mr. Barasa from the bank," Moses said.

"Yeah, I remember him." Amy answered. "What brings you here, Mr. Barasa?"

"I asked him to come," Moses answered. "It's about that movie they made."

"*Jambo*," Mr. Barasa said, extending his hand.

"*Jambo sana*," Amy dutifully replied, shaking his hand.

"Moses says you helped him organise his finances. He's done a very good job of paying off the loan."

"Thank you," Amy said, knowing with certainty that Mr. Barasa had not come all the way from Kakamega to thank Moses for getting ahead on his payments.

"I have good news. People at our office in Chicago liked the video we made of Moses. They want to do more filming, but in America this time. It would be a wonderful experience for the boy, and we would look after him, take care of everything. He'll meet others like himself, coming from other countries, and one of them will be used to promote the bank all over the world next year."

The eye for which Amy had earned her nickname was twitching double-time, as evidence of her concern over this decision. She could see by Moses' face that he was overjoyed at what Mr. Barasa was saying. To her, it sounded a little *too* good; and she could not escape that bad feeling she had about anything to do with banks.

"The bank will pay for everything. We'll buy him new clothes, and he'll stay at a nice hotel in Chicago," Barasa continued. "Moses says he doesn't have a guardian, so we thought we should run this by you first. He says you're his best friend." The twitch slowed, but only slightly.

"How long would he be away? What about his sister... Rosy? He doesn't even have a passport." Questions flooded in, mostly negative ones, like Amy was looking for a good excuse to call off the trip.

"I know someone who can fast track a passport, and we'll *pay* you to look after his sister, if you would be so kind. Moses will only be away two weeks... maximum."

Amy was through with Karla, so she quickly washed her hands over a basin, in a stream of water from a plastic pitcher. She dried them on her dress as she entered the room where Moses and his friend were still standing.

"Please take a seat, and tell me about this," she said.

They all sat down.

The bank manager explained the need for more people to invest with the micro-bank. It would make funds available to help others like Moses, who wanted to start small businesses in developing countries. Shareholders did not receive as much on their investments with his bank, but they had the satisfaction of knowing that their money was being used to help people who would never be able to get a loan from traditional banks.

Branches all over the world had been asked, he explained, to watch for customers who would be a good advertisement for what the bank was trying to do. The amateur video that Mr. Barasa had made of Moses was one of three that had been chosen, and one of those three people would be named "customer of the year". If he was successful, people in many countries would hear Moses' story, about how he had been able to support his younger sister, despite his disability and despite being without parents, all because the micro-bank had helped him get a bike... a ten-speed... to earn a living and pay off the loan. The fact that he was paying off his loan in half the allotted time would, according to the bank manager, impress the judges in Chicago even more.

"I don't know..." said Amy. "It's not really up to me to decide. Things are going so well for the boy right now. He's worked very hard to get that loan paid off. This could just take him away from what he's doing here."

"It's only two weeks, Winky," Moses pleaded.

"Would you like to see what we filmed?" Mr. Barasa asked. "I have a copy in my vehicle."

"Can we, Winky?" Moses asked.

"Yeah, sure, that would be fine," Amy replied. "Will it run off a car battery? It's all the power we have."

"We can watch it on my laptop," Mr. Barasa said, as he stood to leave.

"What do you think about this, Moses?" Amy asked when Barasa was out of earshot. "Are you sure you want to go to another country? Things would be very different for you over there. I don't think you'd like it."

"Oh, I do want to go, Winky," Moses assured her. "Me, I want to see America... what it's like! Even if it's a mis-appointment, I'll be back before two weeks."

"Who would look after you?"

"Winky, no one looks after me now!" he laughed. "You think I need someone to bodyguard me? And these people are *rich*! They'll take care of me. Look at Mr. Barasa!" He pointed out the front window where the bank manager was just leaving his vehicle to return to the house. "See, that's a four-wheel drive he's got. New as a hot loaf of bread! The bank gave it to him."

Mr. Barasa re-entered the house with a computer bag over his shoulder. The bag itself was impressive, with compartments for everything, and so was the computer. He carefully lifted it out of the bag, put it on the coffee table, and then slipped a DVD in the slot on the side. A moment later, he had it playing the film clip that had been prepared for his head office. It was edited, of course, to include the best parts of what they had filmed.

Moses, who had not yet seen the film himself, watched with as much interest as Amy, who was genuinely curious about what her young friend had become involved in. Jo-Jo wandered over to the table and needed to be restrained from interfering with the computer.

"Me, I was in big troubles," Moses was saying at the start of the promotional clip. "I mean really big. And then I got this loan and it... it... revegetated me!" Then he just grinned his biggest grin for the camera, and held it.

There were pictures of Moses waiting at the bike stand with the other drivers, a scene with a customer getting on his bike, then one with him riding off with the customer on the back of the bike. Over all of these, Moses' voice could be heard as he explained his situation.

"Me and my sister didn't have no one to look out for us when my mother died. We was just like that: no work and no food. But when the loan came, even I got a bike, a ten-speed. This is it here. I can't get started properly on a one-speed; but in a low gear on *this* bike, it's easy as cake." For the last few words the camera shifted back to where Moses was showing off his new bike. The image dropped down to a closeup of the gear sprockets.

Then it jumped forward to where he was letting his customer off at the destination, and the customer was fishing in his pocket for some money. The camera zoomed in on the money as it was handed over.

"Now we have food and even we have some extra for stormy times," he said as the final footage rolled.

The clip finished with a repeat of the final words of the first scene: "It... it revegetated me!"

Moses' talent for using original words must have played some part in them picking him. But his total disregard for the obvious handicap of having only one arm was the clincher. People could see for themselves what a difference the loan had made to his life, and it would surely inspire more wealthy Westerners to invest in the bank, which boasted that it was not a charity... "just a way of helping others help themselves."

"When would you want him to go?" Amy asked, as the twitch returned to her eye.

"We can have the passport by next week," Mr Barasa said. "They want him in Chicago by June 15. They're planning a big dinner for some of our investors. Moses will be a special guest."

Amy did not want to offend the bank manager, but she had to be true to her conscience; so she turned to Moses. "You know, boy, I can't tell you what to do," she said. "I'm not your mother; but truth is, I don't feel good about this. I hope you'll pray about it, and make a wise decision."

Amy often talked about praying like that. As if Moses just telephoned God every time he made a decision. He never quite knew what she expected him to do, but at least he knew when she did that, she wasn't going to stop him. Most of the time she was happy with his decisions too, so, in his mind, it wasn't such a big deal if she wasn't happy this once.

"Yeah, I'll go!" he said, turning to Mr. Barasa after only the slightest pause to represent "praying about it". Amy seemed more disappointed with his haste than with the decision itself; but she said nothing.

Chapter 7--Culture Shock

The trip started nicely: a ride in Mr. Barasa's four-wheel drive to Kisumu, then an overnight journey on the train with one of Mr. Barasa's assistants, who was there to keep him company. Moses especially liked the train ride. He had started to order *matumbo* in the dining car when his companion told him he could have chicken instead, because the bank would be paying for it. And what chicken it was! So soft and easy to eat!

In Nairobi, the assistant accompanied Moses to the airport, and left him in the care of a flight attendant.

"Is this your first plane trip?" she asked.

"Yes," he answered, with enthusiasm showing in his eyes as well as his voice. "I'm doing bank business."

She accompanied him through all the boarding procedures, even leading him to a window seat on the plane before other passengers were allowed to board. She offered to put his little bag of clothes and personal items in the overhead compartment, but he wanted to keep it under his seat, where he could protect it from theft.

A young Kenyan couple came and sat beside him. They smiled at him, but seemed more intent on talking with each other.

When all the other passengers were in their seats, there was a video about what to do if the plane should crash. Moses listened intently. He had never heard of planes crashing, and now he was afraid. He looked out the window as they taxied toward the runway, wondering if it was too late to get off.

His left hand tightened on the armrest and the stump of his right arm bent tightly at the elbow as the captain tested the engines. Never before had he heard such noise. Surely the plane was going to explode!

Then they started to accelerate. Moses tried to pretend he was riding in a bus, but then the direction changed and the plane was lifting off the ground. They were in the air, and climbing steeply. There was nothing to support them. They could fall at any moment! What a foolish decision he had made, to put his life at risk like this!

The young woman on the aisle had noticed that something was wrong, and she grabbed a paper bag from a pocket on the seat in front of her just in time to pass it across for Moses to use. He wretched up what was left of the wonderful breakfast he had enjoyed on the train that morning.

A moment later the seatbelt sign went off, and a stewardess rushed to assist the boy. He was led to a rest room, where he could clean himself up. But inside the tiny room there were more problems. He needed to relieve himself, but there was no hole in the floor for doing that. There was a very big bowl with a cover on it, however, and so Moses opened the cover and stood on the sides of the bowl to use it in that way. His good arm slipped when there was a sudden shift in the plane, and one foot plunged into the bowl.

The frightened one-armed passenger did what he could to clean himself with some papers in the toilet, before the stewardess knocked and told him that he needed to return to his seat because of turbulence.

Moses was seated in the first row of the economy section, and so he was offered lunch before anyone else. He had saved up a few hundred shillings to take with him, but he knew they would not go far. There was no one from the bank to pay for the meal, so he refused it and reached under his seat to get some of the sweet biscuits that he had picked up at the railway station in Nairobi.

There were a few moments of confusion before the couple next to him pointed out (in Swahili, to save him embarrassment) that the meals were free. By this time they themselves had their meals in front of them, and were being offered wine to go with it.

"Please, Madam, can I have a meal now?" Moses asked, raising his left hand toward the stewardess.

"Yes, certainly. Chicken or beef?" She asked.

"Chicken, please," he said. "But please, I cannot drink that wine."

The stewardess smiled politely and said, "I think you will like the orange juice. Would you like to try some?"

Moses accepted, and was glad he did. The drink was delicious, and it was colder than any soft drink he had ever had in Shinyalu. In the glass were little pieces of glass that seemed to be making the water cold. They were too painfully cold to put in his mouth, but he later learned that they would change to water over time. The food was good, but there was not enough water to wash his hands after eating it all, and he was disappointed that there was no *ugali*.

If you have not had ugali, you will go to bed hungry, is the saying in his part of Kenya.

By the time he finished his meal, Moses was starting to adjust to being up in the air. He could not see the ground, but there was a forest full of fluffy white treetops down below that he stared at for quite some time. He had never seen such huge "trees" before, and as the plane glided slowly over them, he soon fell asleep.

The flight was a direct one, from Nairobi to Chicago, and it arrived very late by local time. Moses was assisted through Customs by a friendly stewardess, then taken out to meet a man named Townsend, who represented the bank. Mr. Townsend had been holding a sign with Moses' name on it. Introductions were made, and the stewardess handed the teenager over, after which he and his host caught a taxi to a hotel. There was so much to see that it was just one big blur for Moses.

He and Townsend had adjoining rooms, so after a few instructions on how to use the TV and work the lights, and after arrangements had been made to meet up for breakfast at eight the next morning, Mr. Townsend excused himself and went to bed. This time his host thought to tell Moses that everything would be free; he could eat whatever he liked at the buffet breakfast in the hotel restaurant, and the bank would pay for it all. It was almost 2am by the time they parted, but back in Kenya it was already the next morning. Moses had slept sufficiently on the plane, and he was so excited by his new surroundings that he could not possibly sleep now.

There had been only a brief introduction to the facilities in the toilet, but Moses was keen to use the shower. It would be fun to wash without using a bucket, in a huge white tank that was almost deep enough to swim in.

There was a strange handle that Mr. Townsend had said would control the shower, so Moses pushed it up and then jumped back as water poured out from a fitting above his head. He quickly undressed and hopped into the shower, but reacted in horror as scalding water hit his body. He bounded out of the tub and soothed his sore skin with a fluffy white towel. There was no way to turn off the handle without reaching through the dangerous water. He had no choice but to leave it running, even though such a waste of water would be a crime in Shinyalu.

His host had shown him how to use the television, and so he turned it on. There were dozens of channels to choose from, but at this hour of the night, most seemed to be selling things, or they featured preachers of various persuasions. Moses would watch each for a minute or two, until he was bored, and then move on to another.

Then he came to one that grabbed his attention. It was a jungle scene. People on the screen seemed to be frightened about something. He snatched a pillow and sat on the floor with his back to the bed, to take in what was happening on the TV.

It wasn't long before he discovered what had scared the people on the screen. In the jungle there were creatures with needle-like teeth and sharp claws, that pounced on people, and devoured them. There were close-ups of the flesh-eating creatures with saliva dripping from their mouths, and he was convinced that they were from a real Chicago jungle. He was frozen in panic, fearing that they might leap out of the screen and attack him right there in the room where he was staying.

When the scene changed, Moses found the courage to approach the TV and change channels. He came to another, where a young man was surrounded by beautiful women, each trying to seduce him. One by one the women engaged in body movements and enough removal of clothing to shock Moses even further. What kind of a country had he come to! Man-eating monsters, and women who take off their clothes for the whole world to see! He was filled with horror and disgust.

Even after turning the television off, he could not get the images of the two movies out of his head. He was too frightened to turn the light off, but eventually dozed off to sleep. But it was not long before he awoke in fear, believing that there were creatures in the room that wanted his blood.

Around seven o'clock in the morning local time, Moses heard noises in the hallway, suggesting that other residents were up and about. He poked his head through the door and then ventured down the hallway toward the restaurant, where he could see that others had already eaten and left.

A table near the front of the restaurant had the remains of four half-finished meals. There were pieces of toast, slices of bacon, fruit, drinks, even two whole eggs. Moses slid into the bench seat behind the table and, after looking around to see if anyone would object, he started to sample the food. One plate had been cleaned up by the hungry scavenger, and he had moved by another when a hotel employee came over to assist him.

"What is your room number?" she asked.

Moses remembered, because there had been a joke about it being unlucky when they checked in. "Thirteen," he said.

"You may leave these," she explained sweetly. "I'll dispose of them. Just help yourself to whatever you like over at the buffet."

"But who will eat this?" Moses asked.

"No one. I'll throw it out."

"Then I will eat it. This food is delicious!" he said with enthusiasm. "It must not be wasted."

"But you're entitled to *fresh* food. Someone else has been eating here," the waitress continued, turning her nose up a bit at Moses' resistance.

"This food is perfectly fabulous," Moses replied. "Why did they leave it? Surely, we cannot throw it away!"

"But you could become sick. Others have been eating it."

Moses struggled to keep from laughing. How could anyone become sick from eating such perfect food in such a clean restaurant, "If you like, I will not eat that toast... the one with a bite out of it. But look at this egg. It is totally untasted. *Waste not. Want not.* I will eat it."

Moses' demeanour was friendly but firm. The young waitress backed away, in search of a supervisor to assist her in dragging the boy away from the leftovers. Before she returned, however, Moses had finished off what was on the table and was on his way back to his room.

Chapter 8--A Scanner Phone

His victory in the restaurant gave Moses more confidence when he was back in his room. While he waited for Mr. Townsend to wake up, he checked the water in the shower. It was cold now, and so it was safe to turn it off. Then he tried the television once more.

Again he got one of those channels where people phone in and order things at special prices.

"This is just the thing for small businesses," said a heavily made-up woman, holding up what appeared to be a mobile phone. "You've seen them advertised for prices up to a thousand dollars, but today we're offering them to the first 100 callers for just $199."

"Tell us what's so special about it," said the woman's sidekick, a man in his thirties who was doing his best to convince the audience that he had never seen such a thing before in his life.

"It's not just a cell phone. See here," and the camera zoomed in on the tiny piece of hardware that the woman was holding, "It has a built-in scanner, so you can do microchip transactions wherever you happen to be. And the phone itself has an RFID chip so that if it's lost or stolen, you can track it... even if the sim card is switched."

People everywhere had been getting tiny microchip implants injected under the skin on the back of their hands. Moses knew several even in Shinyalu who had the implants. By typing costs into a scanner, these people could complete a business transaction with just a wave of their microchipped hand in front of a scanner. Funds would instantly jump from one person's account to the other's.

Most of the big shops in Kakamega had scanners at the checkout now, and even some of the little ones in the village had them. Moses had heard of one *matatu* driver who had a pocket scanner, but he doubted that any *boda-boda* drivers in all of Kenya had one yet; they were far too expensive. But $199 was less than half the price that they sold for in Kenya. With one of these, Moses would have less fear of being robbed when taking on passengers late at night, because at least a portion of his takings would be in theft-proof electronic money.

But that wasn't his primary interest. Moses was more interested in what the phone could do for his business. People with microchip implants still needed to carry some cash if they travelled by *boda-boda*. But if he had a scanner, Moses could offer his customers a cashless *boda-boda* service... possibly the first one in Kenya.

When Mr. Townsend knocked on the door for breakfast, all the boy wanted to talk about was the scanner.

"Would the bank give me a loan to get one? If I buy one here, will it work in Kenya? How do I get one like the one on TV? It *will* increase business, won't it?"

Mr. Townsend was impressed, and assured Moses that there was no need to buy through the television promoters. He would be able to get Moses a better price through the bank itself. Just leave it with him.

At breakfast, Mr. Townsend was surprised that Moses ate so little, but he put it down to the boy's excitement about being in a new country. Over the meal they discussed plans for the week.

There would be a limousine tour of Chicago right after breakfast, and a meeting with some bank executives for lunch. That evening, after an afternoon rest at the hotel, they would be attending a dinner, where the winner in the competition for customer of the year would be announced. The rest of the week would be taken up with filming for all three contestants, since the bank planned to use all of them in their promotions, even though one would be singled out as the primary symbol for their work. Then there would be two more days of sightseeing and entertainment before they all returned to their home countries.

The other two contestants were staying at the same hotel, and so they all met up in the lobby as they waited for the limousine. When the limo arrived, and they stepped outside the hotel, Moses was almost swept away by the strongest wind he had ever experienced. His horror at being in a such a strange environment returned for just a moment; but when they were all seated inside the limousine, and Mr. Townsend was passing around iced soft drinks, he quickly forgot his fears. All three visitors were blown away by the VIP treatment they were receiving. It more than compensated for the winds for which Chicago was famous.

Lack of sleep overnight took much of the edge off the morning's activities. The drive around Chicago, and the luncheon were little more than a blur, and Moses was ready to do some serious sleeping long before the scheduled rest period in the afternoon. He had to force himself awake at 6pm when Mr. Townsend came to help with preparations for the evening.

"Here, drink this. It'll help you stay awake," he said as he offered Moses an iced tea drink from the machine in the hall. Moses did not have to be asked twice. He was becoming hooked on icy cold drinks.

"Will I be saying anything tonight?" he asked.

"Only if you win, and then you just need to thank the people who brought you here," said Mr. Townsend. "Why? Are you worried?"

"No. What you said is what I strongly want to say," Moses smiled, as he splashed cold water from the sink onto his face, "Me, I want to thank someone. Can I thank you?"

"I'm just one of the little people," Mr. Townsend said humbly. "No, the people to thank are the ones who run the bank, like the people you met at lunch today."

That night, at the banquet, Moses was ocated at a table to the right of the head table, along with some prominent shareholders.

Moses instinctively picked up his chicken with his left hand, then noticed that he was the only one doing it. He put it back on the plate and contemplated how to cut it the way the others were doing. It was nearly impossible with only one hand. But then the man sitting on his left picked his chicken up with his hands too. He smiled and nodded for Moses to do the same.

"Is the food different to what you eat in Kenya?" asked the man, who said his name was Ray. Ray was tall and handsome, and wore a white dinner jacket.

"Mmm... a little," said Moses. "We mostly eat *ugali*."

"What's *ugali*?" asked Ray.

"*Ugali* is..." He paused. "It is food made from maize. It is just *ugali*."

"Tell me about Kenya. What do you like most about living there?" Ray asked.

Moses could not speak for a moment. How could he know what he liked about Kenya when he had nothing with which to compare it? Then he came up with this:

"Me, I like that the people like me in Kenya," he said. "Lots of people. And I know them, too," he added.

"I think people will like you here, Moses, when you get to know us," Ray answered.

Ray was about fifty years old, and Moses liked him already.

"Do you work for the bank?" Moses asked.

"No, I'm one of the people who puts money in the bank," Ray answered. "What can you tell me about the bank in Kenya?"

Again Moses had to struggle for an answer.

"The bank... it helped me," he said. "But I don't know other people. Oh, I know Mr. Barasa! He has a new car and a new computer from the bank. In Kenya, all people want to work for NGOs, because then you get a new car and they pay you big money. One day, I want to work for an NGO."

"But the bank and other non-government organisations are not there just to give away cars, Moses. They go there to help the people of Kenya help themselves."

"Then can you give me a computer like Mr. Barasa has?" Moses asked unashamedly.

Ray blushed as he spoke. "The microbank does not give things away, Moses. People must work for what they get... like you have done with your bicycle."

"Who paid for Mr. Barasa's car and for his computer?" the boy asked.

"That comes from the money that people pay back to the bank," Ray explained. "I guess *you* paid for Mr. Barasa's car, Moses. You and many other Kenyans whom the bank has helped."

"Oh, so the bank is not helping us; we are helping the bank. Is that right?"

Ray chuckled softly. "You could put it that way. Maybe we are each helping the other."

"And this food... the hotel... the big long car... Did we pay for that too?"

"Moses, please understand that we don't live like this all the time. This is something special that we put on for you and for the other contestants."

"But we *did* pay for it, didn't we? We and the other people from our countries? Don't we pay for it by giving you back more than you give us? Isn't that how your business works."

"Well, yes, that *is* how business works, isn't it? But all of these people here," and he waved his arm around the room, "could make more money by investing in other banks... the ones that will not give loans to people like yourself. We make a *little* bit of money from you, but we do not make as much money as we could make from other investments."

"That's good," Moses said with little enthusiasm; and then he suddenly lost interest in the conversation.

After a short pause, Ray tried again to say something that would foster friendship between the two cultures. "I have heard that there are many orphans in Kenya. Do you know any other orphans?"

Moses laughed as though Ray had told a joke.

"They are all over my village," he said, "hundreds of them. Most live with grandparents, but some do like Rosy and me. We live on the land that our father owned, and we do it *independently*."

"Did your father die from AIDS?" Ray asked.

"Me, I don't want to talk about it," Moses replied calmly. He preferred to be seen as an orphan than to go into details about his parents.

"Okay, I understand." (But, of course, he did not.) "What *would* you like to talk about?"

Moses thought for a moment, as he pushed the remnants of his meal around his plate. Then he spoke:

"Me, I want to talk about why do Americans drink so much tea?"

"I don't know why we drink so much tea," Ray said with surprise. "I guess we just like it."

"But in Western Kenya we do not have enough land to grow food for ourselves. Big tea companies buy our land to grow tea. And then they bring it here to throw it away." He pointed to half-finished iced tea glasses being cleared away by a waitress. "Why do Americans not grow their own tea?"

Ray was impressed. He had been told that Moses was only sixteen years old (although the boy was really much younger, and the bank in Kenya had lied about his age). Nevertheless, for his age, whatever it might be, Moses' grasp of economics was amazing.

"I guess we are just too greedy," Ray admitted. "Maybe that is why we invest in micro-banks, so we can make up for what we have taken." He smiled humbly.

"But with your micro-bank, you take *more* money from us. How will that help?"

They were back to that sore point again.

"With your bicycle, you will be able to make money... much more than what you gave to us for the loan," Ray explained. "Isn't that true?"

"But even if I make very much money, me, I can only buy maize from other Kenyans. In all of Kenya, it will not give us more maize. If there is not enough food, then all the money I can make will not stop some other Kenyan from being hungry. We need more food, Mr. Ray, and not more money."

"You know, Moses, I never did think of it like that," Ray admitted. The boy had opened his eyes; surely, the only way to overcome hunger was to send food, or just to stop using so much of the world's land to grow non-essentials like tea, coffee, and tobacco for the West.

"Do you think I can get your address?" Ray asked. "I would like to keep in touch with you when you go back to Kenya."

"Sure," Moses said, and he scribbled his name and

address on a napkin: Moses Chikati, Shinyalu Post Office, Western Kenya. "Can you send me stamps?"

"You mean used stamps?"

"Yes, from America. Can you send some? I can give them to my friend, Winky." Moses knew a little shop in Kakamega that would buy the stamps, and it was customary to ask foreigners for stamps as a form of donation.

"I travel a lot, so I can send you stamps from other countries too. How would you like that?"

Moses barely had time to express his pleasure at the suggestion when the master of ceremonies tapped on the microphone and started the evening's business.

There were boring speeches about the work of the micro-bank, and a report to the shareholders, and then they showed the three videos that had been made about Moses and the other two customers of the micro-bank.

Shanti was from India, and she had used a single sewing machine (operated in shifts, around the clock by women from her village) to develop a dress-making business that was now exporting to exclusive American shops. Rapalo was from Fiji, and he had invented a simple solar cooker that promised to save significantly on fuel consumption in his own country, and maybe in others as well. Then there was Moses. He felt insignificant, given that the others had already achieved success in their fields... successes that had an impact far beyond their own village and even beyond their own country. Moses was just a humble teenage *boda-boda* driver, who had only finished repaying his debt one month ago.

The world president of the bank then gave a speech. He said how impressed he was by Shanti's ability to organise and motivate women in her community, and also by the high quality of the work they produced... quality which had attracted the attention of dress shops in America. He went on to say that Rapalo's invention, while still in its early marketing stages, was one that could have a great impact on the world, at a time when fuel consumption was at the forefront of everyone's minds.

And finally he came to Moses.

"When I think of what it is that our bank does most consistently and most effectively," he said, "I think that it gives simple, hard-working people a chance to survive, in a world where circumstances are often stacked against them. Moses Chikati has not only been caring for himself and his younger sister while paying off his loan, but he has paid the loan back in half the time that the bank had allowed. His hard work, thrift, and cheerful nature are sure to take him far. I am pleased to announce that Moses Chikati will feature as this year's symbol of what our bank stands for: good people helping themselves. Moses, can you come forward to receive your certificate!"

It was still sinking in that he had actually won the competition when Ray reached over to shake Moses' left hand. "Good work, Moses! You did it; and remember, you helped pay for all of this! Go get your prize."

Moses left his seat and walked toward the back of the head table, where he extended the stump of his right forearm in response to the president's extended right hand. Then he lifted slightly on his toes to face the mike.

"Me, I want just to thank the people who paid to bring us here and feed us and show us around at this big celebration. Two of them are here tonight: Thank you, Ms Shanti, and thank you Mr. Rapalo. You see, when we paid our money back to the bank, even we gave a little extra, and my friend Ray, he was telling me that we are helping him and his friends by giving them a little more than they gave to us. I know I did not give enough to pay for what I have received at this thing here tonight, but *multitudes* of people like Shanti and Rapalo, from many countries, give a little each, and already this is what we made." He swung his good arm in a proud semi-circle in front of himself.

"We did good, didn't we?" And he finished with a huge grin, as the audience laughed and clapped in response.

Then the bank president returned to the microphone.

"I almost forgot," he said.

"The board had a special meeting this afternoon, and we heard that Moses wanted to buy a scanner phone, so that he can become the first *boda-boda* driver in Kenya to introduce scanning. Moses, we have decided to give you this phone as part of your prize. You are quite right, that we are only giving back to you and all of our other customers around the world, something that you collectively paid for yourselves.

"Use it with our best wishes!" And he reached out to shake Moses' hand a second time, this time remembering to extend his left hand.

Chapter 9--Relations with Amy

"Oh, Moses, no, no! What have I done?" Amy covered her face with her hands, and bowed her head in anguish, as Moses looked on in confusion. He had just been showing her his new scanner phone.

"What do you mean, Amy? What did I do wrong?"

Amy peeked out from behind her fingers, and then dropped her hands altogether.

"God forgive me. I never told you, Moses. Those microchips... They're evil!"

Moses had never heard Amy talk like this before, and he was shocked. "What do you mean *evil*? They're just microchips."

"The Bible says so," Amy began.

"The Bible?" Moses almost shouted, knowing instinctively that it wasn't just the Bible that Amy was referring to. This had Josephat written all over it. "Microchips weren't even *existed* in Bible times, Winky! You been talking to Josephat, haven't you?" he asked.

"Moses, even in my church back in Australia, they talked about the microchip. We didn't call it like that then, but we knew something was coming... something people could use to buy and sell. It's called the Mark in the Bible... the Mark of the devil."

Moses was deeply offended; but he just sighed and waited for Amy to finish.

"The Bible says anyone who gets the Mark will be punished real bad by God, Moses. It says his *wrath* will be on them. Do you want that, son?"

Amy reached for a Bible and started to look up the passage that she was referring to. As she did, Moses launched into his defence.

"Winky, *I'm* not getting a microchip. I'm just using the phone for people who already have it. Do you think God is going to punish me for that?"

"Here it is," said Amy, ignoring his question.

"*He causes everybody, both small and great, rich and poor, free and bond, to receive a mark in their right hand, or in their forehead*... That's the devil, Moses, or at least the son of the devil. It's the Antichrist who does that!"

"You're not listening, Winky. I don't *have* the mark. I got no right arm, see!" And he held up his stump.

"Yeah, true. I can see that," Amy said, sounding perplexed as she glanced down at the Bible. She blinked a few times and then she pleaded, "Well... promise me you won't ever get it."

"Winky, how can I? I got no right arm."

Moses knew secretly that he had not promised her anything. The passage said something about a mark on the forehead. If it happened that there was a microchip for the forehead, he would be less worried about getting it than he would be about telling a lie to Winky. Because he technically hadn't promised, he still felt that he had left his options open.

It's all Josephat's fault, he thought to himself, secretly hating the man who had come between him and his best friend, Winky.

To everyone else, Moses was already a celebrity... not because of the posters and TV ads that would soon be shown around the world (People in the village had no idea about that yet.) but just because he had been overseas. He had been to America.

So why couldn't Amy show a little more respect too?

Moses had only arrived back in Shinyalu the day before, and he hadn't yet returned to work. When he did, the following day, he was the center of attention; business had never been better. Most locals still didn't have the microchip, but those who did went straight to him as soon as they learned that he had a scanner. It was just as well that he had shared customers with the other *boda-boda* drivers previously, because he was clearly taking business from them now. And it continued that way for a long time after.

Amy made a few attempts to broach the topic of the scanner, but Moses just smiled and assured her that he had heard what she was saying, and that he was thinking about it... which he wasn't really.

Ray had asked the bank for the cell phone number, and then called Moses two days after he got back. The subject of the new cell phone came up, and Moses complained... but only a little... about Amy's attitude. Ray was sympathetic. He supported Moses in making his own decision, but coached him on being tactful about it too. Moses liked having a male to turn to and SMS's became a regular thing between the two of them after that.

Then, a few weeks later, Amy said she wanted to "talk" with him. He had stopped reportng to her, now that the loan was repaid, and he had his own bank account. But he had developed good habits, and he and Rosy were quickly saving up money to start construction on a real house... one with brick walls and an iron roof.

When Amy first mentioned a "talk", Moses tensed up, thinking that he was going to be in trouble for something. But that soon changed.

"I need your help," she began, and Moses looked surprised.

"You need *my* help?" he asked, pointing at himself with his good left hand.

"We got problems here with the children, son. Some of the people who give to help us have stopped giving. It happens with most missionaries over time; people move away, die, or just forget about what's happening way over here. So they have to go home from time to time... to get new supporters.

"But I got no one to mind the children if I leave. I'm not part of a proper church; it's just me and the kids."

Moses was wondering what all of this had to do with him. Was she asking him to give her the money he and Rosy had been saving? He could maybe give a little, but not enough to save the orphanage.

"I have a friend in Australia," she said. "A Quaker, like the people here, 'cept they're different in some ways. He heard of our work through a pastor in Kakamega who went to Australia for a big Quaker meeting five years ago.

"The man's name is Kyme. Kyme has been asking me to come and talk to Quakers in Australia, to see if they can help with the work here. He said he'd pay my way if I could come over and talk."

And then Amy paused, like she was waiting for Moses to guess what this had been leading to. He thought for a while but surely she was not going to ask him to run the orphanage! Even Benje wasn't old enough to do that! So he waited to see what she would say.

"You did so well on your trip to America," she said. And then it started to dawn on Moses what she was suggesting. "The bank thinks you'll do a good job making people want to give. Do you think you could do something like that for me? In Australia?"

Moses was glowing. He had moved from fearful thoughts about being in trouble, to being asked if he could "help" by taking another trip overseas, this time to Australia. What a great offer!

"You really want me to go to Australia? for you?" he asked incredulously. "That would be... *momentous*, When do you want me to go?"

"I haven't thought that far ahead," Amy admitted. "But we need something pretty quick. You have your passport, and Kyme said he can send a ticket whenever I like. We just need to go over some questions they may ask about the work here."

"Can you watch Rosy again?" Moses asked.

"Of course!" Amy exclaimed; but it encouraged her to see Moses thinking about his sister's welfare.

Chapter 10--Australia

It took a further two weeks to get things organised, but by early September, Moses was on a plane headed for yet another part of the world.

It was winter in Australia when he arrived, and although the weather in Sydney is mild by world standards, it was still the coldest weather Moses had ever endured, and he found it a painful experience. The thermometer had dipped below ten degrees Celcius the day before Moses arrived, and it stayed that way for most of the week that he was there. The young Kenyan described it as "full body pain" in a text-message to Amy after he arrived; but he assured her that it was not enough to stop him from accomplishing his goal for the trip: He was going to secure financial support for Amy and the kids. He was, of course, much more prepared for cultural differences this time, as a result of his previous jaunt to America.

Because Kyme lived a hundred miles north of Sydney (and because he was a bachelor, with no experience of children) he had arranged to have Moses stay with a Quaker family in a Sydney suburb while he himself stayed at the meeting house across town. Moses thought this sounded a hundred times better than a hotel room on his own. But in reality it was a little disappointing.

The "children" were two brothers in their early twenties, who didn't have much time for him or for their mother either. The mother, Deb, was divorced and worked as a psychologist at the local welfare department.

"Young people need freedom to live their own lives," Deb explained when her sons did not turn up for the first meal with her, Kyme, and Moses. Kyme had met Moses at the airport earlier in the day, and brought him back to the house. He had hung around all day while Moses rested up from the trip. After dinner Kyme would be off to the meeting house, returning in the morning to take Moses to his appointment with Quaker Service Australia.

"The boys often stay out all night, but perhaps you can meet them tomorrow," Deb suggested.

Earlier that day, on the trip back from the airport, Kyme had briefed Moses on the meeting with Quaker Service. "Don't expect too much," he had warned. "Quakers have plenty of money, but there are a lot of rules that keep them from giving practical help. I'm just hoping that your presence will soften their hearts a little."

"You think I got enough charismatics for them?" Moses asked cheerfully.

"I hear you won the banks over," said the chubby old man with a twinkle in his eyes. "Just stay positive and don't let them rattle you."

Kyme explained that he personally thought faith of any sort involved sacrifice. "But don't say the word *sacrifice* around them tomorrow," he warned. "It's not the way most Quakers think these days. If they decide to help, it won't take much sacrifice anyway. Amy says she only needs $500 a month to cover all her expenses. That's nothing for Australians. One Quaker would make more than that in a day or two."

Kyme listed two concepts that Moses *should* try to include in his spiel: *Indigenous*, and *sustainable*.

"*You're* indigenous," said Kyme. "And that's good. But Amy isn't, at least not in Kenya. If they ask about her, tell them that she's trying to find her roots in Kenya. Do you know about that?"

"Yeah, she told me," Moses replied. "She talks fluid Luhya, you know. So we take her as one of us."

"Just don't say that she's a missionary," Kyme warned. "Quakers think missionaries are just preachers. It would be too hard to convince them otherwise."

Moses screwed up his face to express puzzlement, but he said nothing.

"What does *sustainable* mean?" he asked.

Kyme cleared his throat and began. "It means that it can keep on going without hurting the environment or using up resources."

Moses cocked his head to one side and listened intently for more.

"Like if your village is using more trees than they can re-grow, it can't go on forever, can it? So we would say that it's not sustainable."

"Can't we just import stuff?" Moses asked.

"Not the way Friends see it," Kyme replied as they pulled into Deb's driveway.

They walked up the path to the front door while Kyme continued: "Sustainability is going to be the hardest part about asking for help. Amy has to show that sooner or later she can support herself... become sustainable."

"Oh, I see," said Moses. "So we won't have to import more money! Don't worry. She put something like that in her informations... some business propositions."

The conversation ended when they were inside, as Moses became distracted by the many furnishings, wall hangings, and bookshelves around the house.

Later, after Deb had arrived home, and while they were eating dinner together, Moses shared some of what he had been thinking about during the afternoon.

"Are Quakers indigenous?" he asked them both.

"What on earth do you mean by that?" Deb replied. Kyme just smiled, as he sensed where Moses might be heading with this.

"Quakers like indigenous things, isn't that right?" Moses asked. "So are Quakers indigenous?"

"We have a few Aboriginal members," said Deb, with a puzzled glance at Kyme. "But you don't have to be indigenous to be a Quaker. Who told you that?"

"No one told me," Moses answered, sensing that he could be causing embarrassment for Kyme. "I'm just trying to understand this word *indigenous*."

"Indigenous is like natural... stuff that was there from the earliest times. Indigenous plants, indigenous languages, indigenous people. Quakers think we should keep things the way they were." Deb relaxed as Moses appeared to be agreeing with what she was saying.

"So it's more than just people?" Moses asked rhetorically. "it must be hard to keep everything how it was."

"We can't undo what's been done," Deb explained. "But we can try to preserve what still remains. Friends are very active in doing this."

"Can you tell me about global warming?" Moses asked, after a short pause. When he saw the surprised look on their faces, he added, "I read about it in a magazine on the coffee table... this afternoon."

"Global warming comes mostly from burning things," Deb explained. She liked being able to teach someone whose mind was so open. "Burning makes carbon dioxide, and if we get too much carbon dioxide, the whole world gets warmer. It could cause flooding and a lot of other environmental problems."

"We burn wood to cook in Kenya. People don't burn wood in Australia, do they?" Moses asked.

"We might be better off if we did," said Kyme. "See, we burn fuel mostly... in our vehicles, but also to make electricity."

"You mean cars make this carbon-oxide stuff too?" Moses asked.

"Yes, *lots* of it," Kyme confessed.

"Do Quakers try to change that too?" Moses asked.

"Yes, we're all trying to use less fuel," Deb put in. "It's very important that we do."

Moses continued to probe. "How do you do that?"

"We take trains and buses when we can. We buy vehicles with smaller engines. We join car pools..."

"But you have three cars," Moses exclaimed. "In Kenya we mostly use bikes. I have a bike."

"Two of the cars belong to my sons," Deb explained. "But *we* have bikes too."

"Do you go to work in the car?" Moses asked. He had seen her return home in it. Now Deb was starting to feel uncomfortable.

"I work almost ten kilometres from here," Deb said. "And I advertised for riders to share, but no one was interested."

"Ten kilometres?" Moses asked rhetorically as he rubbed his chin. "That's how far it is from Shinyalu to Kakamega. Most people walk, but some take the *boda-bodas*. I carry them." And he grinned at Deb.

Deb looked at Kyme, who was smiling too, and then she decided to change the subject. "Let's move into the lounge room," she said. "I'll clear the dishes later."

But Moses was not going to stop. When they were seated, he refused an offer to watch TV.

"When do you use your bikes?" he asked, instead.

"On weekends, mostly, when we go to the mountains. We have some nice bike trails up in the ranges."

"Are the mountains closer than where you work?"

"No, they're farther. We take the bikes on the back of the Toyota. It has a bike rack on it."

"You Quakers have funny ways to stop burning things," Moses said with a nervous giggle that sounded a little like Rosy. Then he picked up the magazine he had been reading earlier, about global warming, and leaned back in the chair to continue reading it.

Chapter 11--Quaker Service

The next day, Moses had breakfast at 8am, before Deb left for work. Kyme was to come for him at nine, and they would go together to the meeting at ten.

Deb was uncomfortable about Moses watching her from the front window as she backed the big station wagon out of the garage, but there was nothing she could do about it.

For his part, Moses just waved and smiled.

When Kyme arrived he shared candidly with Moses:

"You had Deb and me both embarrassed last night," he confessed. "You may not know it, but Deb goes to meeting by train, and I walk to meeting in Newcastle; but I agree, we could be doing more... much more."

"I wasn't trying to humble-ate you," Moses said. "I was really just interested about global warming. I never heard of it in Kenya."

"I see," Kyme said. "I can get you some more articles on the subject, if you like. You can take them back to Kenya with you."

It wasn't clear whether Kyme had changed his plans as a result of what Moses said, because he arrived by car but then parked it at the station and they caught a train to the meeting house in the city.

It seemed that everyone else had arrived early, because the fourteen-year-old and his older companion arrived on time, and still the committee members were all waiting for them. Introductions were made and then they got down to business.

"I asked for this meeting," Kyme explained, "so that young Moses here could tell you something about a project that I have been supporting in Kenya, where there are tens of thousands of orphans as a result of the AIDS epidemic. The woman who I have been sponsoring is not supported by any church or charity, and she has no other source of income. She personally takes care of nine orphans, whom she has raised as if they were her own family. She would have come herself, but she can't leave the children on their own. So she sent Moses here to tell us about what she's doing."

"Are you one of the children from the orphanage?" asked a plump man with grey hair and spectacles.

"It's not really an orphanage," Moses replied. "Just Amy and her kids. Me and my sister, we take care of ourselves. But Amy helps us sometimes."

"If you and your sister are orphans, why isn't she taking care of you?" asked another overweight member of the committee, this one a woman with short black hair and heavy make-up. Just then, Moses looked them over, and noted that all of them were plump, or by Kenyan terms, just plain fat.

"She doesn't *need* to take care of me." he said indignantly. "I have a job, and I take care of myself. But she's having too many complexities just with the kids she has. That's why I'm here... to ask you to help her."

"And what is it that you want us to do for her?" another woman asked, leaning toward him with the widest smile Moses had ever seen.

"Well, she needs some money, mostly for food right now, but if she had a little extra, she wants to build a whole bunch of cages in her yard and grow rabbits. With about a hundred cages, the kids can have meat, and she can sell some to buy clothes and stuff. Then she won't need to ask you for anything more."

Several members of the committee looked knowingly at each other, and then the woman with the short hair volunteered to speak on their behalf.

"Moses, rabbits are not indigenous to Kenya, are they?" she asked.

"No, not in the early days, but we got lots of them now," he said.

"People brought rabbits to Australia many years ago," the woman continued, "and today they're a plague to the farmers. They eat up everything. It only takes a couple of rabbits to escape, and they can upset the whole balance of nature."

"But in Kenya, if rabbits get out, wild animals eat them. They're not a problem, I promise," Moses pleaded.

The committee just looked at him sadly while the reality sunk in. But they were not prepared for his plucky spirit.

"What do Australian Quakers eat?" he asked. And when they did not answer he went on. "Do you eat potatoes? Do you eat carrots? Do you eat chickens?" He was going through the items that he had consumed for tea the night before.

"Are these things indigenous?"

There was an awkward silence, and Kyme struggled to keep from laughing. Then the man who had spoken first, leaned forward across the table as he tried very hard to reach Moses emotionally.

"It's true, we do eat these things, Moses," he said kindly. "But you see, son, we have been doing it too long now to change. It's different with you. You're asking us to start up something... to support something with Quaker money, that is likely to become a threat to the environment. We just can't do it."

Moses paused only for a few seconds, because he had a different approach that he wanted to try... one that he was sure would pass their indigenous concerns.

"That's okay, then," he said. "Amy has another idea... one about bees and honey. We have bees in the Kakamega forest... little ones that don't sting.... they're African bees... *indigenous*, true and truly" he said, followed by a big grin. And then he went on. "Amy has a friend who knows how to start up beehives, and if we can build a bunch of them, Amy saze she can make enough honey to sell to the whole village. No one has ever done it like a business before. Some people even use the honey for medicine, so I know they'll buy it."

The committee listened intently, obviously impressed with the idea. They asked a few questions, and Moses had the right answers for everything. Finally, they asked him and Kyme to step out into the hallway while they discussed the proposal amongst themselves.

"That was excellent," Kyme said to Moses when they were alone in the hallway; and he shook his hand enthusiastically. "Now we just have to wait and see."

They were there quite a while when the woman with the short hair poked her head out the door and asked Kyme to come in.

"Shall I bring Moses with me?" he asked.

"No, it won't be long. He can wait here," she said.

Kyme went in and Moses waited anxiously. The door and walls were thick, but he thought he could hear some raised voices, and that made him nervous.

Then the door burst open and Kyme came out.

"Come with me," he said to Moses, and reached his right hand toward Moses' good arm, while his left hand pointed toward the street outside. Moses had no choice but to follow him.

"What happened?" he said when they were outside of the building.

"They were never going to help you in the first place," he said angrily. "The whole meeting was a farce. They let me bring you all the way over here for nothing."

"What do you mean? How do you know that?" Moses asked, feeling the anger in Kyme's voice.

"They said your request was a good one. It fit all of the criteria for a grant. But they said that the bottom line is that it needs to be made to someone in London. British Quakers are responsible for projects in Kenya, they say, and Australia supports work in Uganda."

Moses just listened, bug-eyed.

"They could have told me that right at the start, but they didn't want to hurt my feelings. They wanted me to think they were giving you a fair hearing. A fair hearing... hah! They were never going to help you!"

It was about then that Kyme started thinking beyond his own hurt and to realise that his anger could spread to Moses and, of course, to Amy, since they had as much reason to feel disappointed as he did. He looked across at Moses as they strode toward Central Railway Station.

"Don't worry. Amy will get her money," he said. "I can cover it myself. I don't know why I even bothered asking them in the first place. I'll go to the bank tomorrow, and get out $6,000. That's enough for a whole year. And Amy can raise rabbits or make honey or sell bloody chocolate lamingtons, for all I care!"

Moses decided right then that Kyme was definitely the best Christian he had ever known, even though Kyme himself had never said anything about what he believed.

"C'mon, you wanna see some of the sites of Sydney before we go back to Deb's place?" he asked.

"Sure," Moses replied.

"There's Chinatown, the museum, the art gallery, or a boat across the harbour to the zoo. Which would you prefer?"

"Oh the boat, for definite sure!" Moses shouted.

And the older man reached out to give him a little hug on the shoulder as they turned toward Circular Quay.

Chapter 12--Back Home

Moses never did meet Deb's sons till the day before he flew out; but all the exciting things he did with Kyme over those next few days more than made up for it. They saw amazing buildings, great exhibitions, and top class sporting events; but the best part was just being with Kyme. His real father was regarded as "dead" because of the murder, but Moses now had two others to take the place, one in America and one here in Australia.

He attended an Australian Quaker "meeting" on Sunday -- the same day that he met Deb's two sons. Kyme had explained that the meeting would be held totally in silence, unless God gave someone something to share with the rest of the meeting. The idea of God talking through someone in the meeting was exciting, and Moses wondered what He would say.

"A whole hour, and all they said was that there's goin' ta be a parade next week?" Moses complained when he was alone with Kyme after the meeting. "That's not a message from God; it's an 'ouncement."

Kyme reminded him that the man who made the announcement had asked Friends to pray for the festival ("Hold it in the light" was how he put it.) because it would be the first time the Gay and Lesbian Mardi Gras was held in September, and organisers were fearful that it would not be as successful as it had been in previous years. Quakers were keen Mardi Gras supporters.

"It's still not a message from God," Moses argued, and Kyme decided not to push the point.

Todd and Michael, Deb's sons, rolled out of bed for a late lunch at her house after the others had returned from the meeting for worship. The boys were polite and friendly, but not particularly interested in Moses or where he was coming from. Moses tried to discuss global warming with them, but they showed little interest apart from some private joke about burning a pot, that Moses could not make sense of.

The brothers left after lunch to meet up with their friends, but Moses didn't mind, because he and Kyme were going to tour a big old sailing ship in Darling Harbour before watching a movie on a screen that was bigger than the biggest house he had ever seen. Kyme said that things on the screen would jump out at them like they were real, and they certainly did! Moses wore special paper glasses to get the effect.

On Monday, Kyme arrived quite early to take him to the airport, for the flight back to Nairobi. Kyme had taken time off work during the previous week, in order to be with Moses and he had to be back in Newcastle by midday. Kyme agreed to send used stamps and to stay in touch by mail and phone. In addition, he gave Moses several hundred dollars in cash for Amy. He placed it in a money belt which Moses could wear under his shirt. The rest of Kyme's gift was sent by electronic transfer.

Without a doubt, it had been the best week of Moses' young life, and he went over and over it in his mind on the way home. He now had two very special friends, and through text messaging he could afford to contact both Kyme and Ray at least once a week.

The welcome from Amy was a huge improvement on her reaction when Moses had returned from Chicago. She actually broke down in tears as she thanked him.

"I don't know why you're thanking me, Amy," he said. "I should be thanking you. You won't believe all the things Kyme and me did." Amy did believe, of course, because she had been raised in Australia; but it was very different for Rosy. Rosy found it hard to even picture what Moses was talking about, much less decide whether or not he had made it up. Nevertheless, he talked about it all for weeks after that, giving Rosy a better picture of what life was like outside of their village.

*   *   *

By December, when Moses turned 15, things were looking very good for him and his sister. Work on the foundation for their new house had begun; they were eating better; and Moses had started taking one day a week off to do "studies". He read everything he could get his hands on, including some magazines that Deb and Kyme had given him just before he left Australia. What he learned through reading the articles on global warming made him something of a local expert on that and other environmental issues, which he often discussed with his customers and other *boda-boda* drivers.

Moses faithfully passed the postage stamps on to Amy, but he treasured the handwritten letters and regular text messages he received from Kyme and Ray, as though they were coming from his own father.

Chapter 13--Josephat Returns

In January, Josephat turned up again, still talking about God destroying those who destroy the earth.

He never stops, Moses thought, wondering how the man could possibly maintain his enthusiasm for something that everyone must know was not going to happen. If anything, Josephat seemed more intense than ever.

For all his skepticism, Moses still felt drawn to leave his post and walk the bike over to where a small crowd was listening to Josephat once again.

"Don't take it, brothers and sisters. Don't take it."

He was talking about the microchip implant, that was growing in popularity.

"It's of the devil," he warned. "Most of you know that already. You don't need me to tell you."

Moses was surprised to hear this. How would the others know what Winky had told him? Perhaps Josephat had been talking about the implant more than he realised. Or did these people know from some other source?

"We know about the *Mark*," said Obadiah, the post master. He had closed the office once again, so he could listen in. "We heard about it in our churches. But is this implant the same thing? Some of us are goin' ta need it just to keep our jobs."

"Same as the Bible saze," Josephat responded. "Can't buy or sell without it. But it comes from the *Beast*... the one who dies and comes back to life again."

"But how're we goin' ta feed our families?" asked a man in the audience.

"Better to ask how're you goin' ta obey God," Josephat replied. "If you can't trust him to feed you and your kids without the Mark, then what kind of God is he anyway?"

"How do *you* pay for things, Josh?" asked someone else. "I never see you using money."

"I do a little," Josephat explained, "but I been *training*. Living simple. Listening to God. Helping other people. Then I just trust God to do the rest. I get by."

"Well, we can't all live like that," Obadiah replied. "We got a scanner in the post office even now, and soon they say it's *all* we're goin' ta have."

Others in the crowd looked at Obadiah in surprise. It was the first they had heard that the microchip might replace cash altogether. Most of them still didn't have an implant.

"I probably wasn't supposed to say that," Obadiah said. "But it's what the memos from Nairobi been telling me. Might still be a few years, though."

Moses wondered what the other *boda-boda* drivers were going to do if that happened. He was thankful that he already had a scanner.

"God's goin' ta destroy them that destroys the earth," Josephat repeated, taking the crowd back to his original point. "Like it or not, that's what I hafta say."

"What does that have to do with scanners and microchips?" asked Obadiah.

"I can't say that I know, but it does," Josephat said, and he stood to leave.

Obadiah re-opened the post office, and the crowd drifted quietly away. But Moses was still interested in Josephat, who was walking away from the markets and in the direction of Winky's house. Sure enough, he kept right on walking until he was out of the village; and then he turned in at the gate in front of Winky's.

Moses followed from a distance on the bike.

* * *

"I'm here to make some inquisitions," the boy said, when Amy had answered the door and asked what brought him there. She smiled kindly and let him in.

"Moses, I think you know Josephat," she said as she offered a seat across from the itinerant preacher. Karla was sleeping on the couch, and Benjie was playing on the floor with some tiny boxes that he had put bottle caps on to make wheels.

"Josephat, this is a young friend of mine. His names are Moses Chikati." Then, after a pause: "So what kind of 'inquisitions' do you want to ask, Moses?"

Moses was not sure what he wanted to ask. "How long before we all need to have the Mark?" he began.

"Can't say," Josephat said. "It was Obadiah who was talkin' 'bout that. Maybe you should talk to him."

But it wasn't Obadiah that was bothering Moses. It was Josephat.

"You say God is going to destroy people. Who? People here in Shinyalu?"

"I don't know for sure," Josephat confessed again. "I don't think it's people right here; but it might be."

More of his confusing double-talk, thought Moses.

"If you want people to believe you, you have to be more, well... *plain* about what you say," Moses lectured.

He knew that what he was about to say was going to hurt Amy, but he wanted to hurt Josephat even more. "You know, even Winky doesn't agree with what you're saying. She doesn't believe in all that end of the world stuff. She told me. Didn't you, Winky?"

It had the desired effect. Josephat looked stunned, and glanced toward Amy, who looked embarrassed.

"But I'm *starting* to believe it, Moses," Amy said calmly. "It just takes a while. Besides, like Josephat says, even *he* doesn't know all of what is going to happen."

"He doesn't know *any* of it, to my way of thinking," Moses said under his breath. "It's just *balderdash.*"

Then he stuck his chest out to emphasise his own confidence, and said, "The people who are destroying the earth are the *rich people*... from places like America and England. They do it by mining, and drilling, and desolating rain forests, and wasting resources. They put poisons into the water and even into the air that we breathe. They're the ones you need to preach at."

He looked straight at the preacher and said, "You don't need to preach your sermons here, Josephat. People in Shinyalu aren't the ones who destroy the earth."

"You may be right," said Josephat, surprising Moses at how easily he had accepted what the boy had just told him. "You seem to know more about it than I do. I just had those words to preach, and the spirit of God burning deep inside of me."

"So if the rich countries are goin' ta be destroyed, why tell it to people in Shinyalu?" Moses asked angrily.

"I can't truly say," Josephat said humbly. "Maybe we just need to *know*... now... before it happens."

"But if you don't even know what's going to happen, then you just end up *confounding* the people," Moses argued.

Josephat said nothing, and Amy shifted uneasily.

"Moses, have you ever thought of throwing out your scanner?" she asked after an awkward silence. "You know, you still could."

"Whatever made you ask that?" Moses said. "I need the scanner for my business. If Obadiah's right, we're *all* goin' ta need them soon."

Amy blinked involuntarily and looked disappointed.

"Winky, you said my job is to take care of Rosy, right? How'm I goin' ta do that, if I don't have a job?"

"I didn't mean it that way, son," she replied. "But I do want to talk to you about Rosy. She's been coming over after school for the past few weeks. She wants to move in with us. Has she said anything to you about it?"

"No way! She never said nothing!" Moses shouted. "Sides, how could you know what she's thinking?"

"She's starting to open up and share things, Moses. I hope you won't get upset with her and scare her, now that she's talking," Amy pleaded.

"You're the one who's upsetting her," Moses argued. "She's exactly OK with me. We're goin' ta have our own house in a year... a brick one, almost as big as yours."

"Moses, Rosy loves you, and she knows you love her; but she wants to come here," and Amy paused before adding, "to help, and to be around the other children."

"You don't even *take* kids like us. I know the rules," Moses said angrily. "You just want to hurt me."

"We don't want to hurt you," Amy replied, as she looked to Josephat for help. "But this is different. Rosy believes God wants her here... to get ready for what's coming."

Moses jumped to his feet, too upset to stay seated. "Get ready for *nothing*!" he shouted. "It's all just talk. That's what I been telling you. Josephat doesn't even know hisself what he's talking about. First he mixed up your head, and now he's doing it to Rosy too. It's not fair. She's all I have!" And he let a tear sneak out before he rubbed his eyes and turned to walk away.

"Son, we don't want to hurt you," Amy pleaded, as she reached out to hug the boy and prevent him from going. The twitich in her eye was one of sheer pain now. "You could come too, if you really wanted." He let her hug him for just a moment, but Amy could feel that he would not come. So she finished by saying firmly, "Boy, if you really love your sister, please don't stop her."

He did not answer. He just shook her hands away from his body and continued on out the door.

When he was out of sight of anyone else, Moses sat down on the side of the road and let the tears flow. He *had* seen a change in Rosy. She was talking more. Amy had indeed worked magic on her. But how could he let her go? How could he live without her?

Chapter 14--Rosy Decides

Moses had little interest in work after the scene with Amy, so he finished earlier than usual that night. When he entered the hut, however, he found it empty. He looked around the *shamba* and could see that Rosy had not been tending the garden as she should have. Then, a few minutes later, she walked up the path. Rosy looked surprised and embarrassed to see him home already.

"You are earlier than me tonight," she said in Luhya, giggling. "Are you sick?"

"Where have you been?" he asked sternly in their mother tongue. "School finished two hours ago."

"I was visiting Winky. She said you came by this afternoon too." And she laughed.

"You can't do the planting and visit Winky at the same time," he said. "We will need the maize just to live when I start buying bricks."

They had already dug foundations for their future home, and the trenches were waiting for the walls to go up.

"Moses, I won't be here," Rosy said. And she neither laughed nor giggled.

So, it was true. She was going to move in with Winky. The options open to him raced through Moses' head before he spoke. He could see they were few.

"You can visit her," he pleaded. "Every day, if you like. But I need you, Rosy. Stay here with me. Please?"

"You don't need me," she said, and the customary laugh returned. "I eat more food than I grow." And she laughed again.

"It's not about food, Rosy." Moses was begging now. "You're my sister... my family. I want to take care of you. I don't want to live here all alone."

Rosy had never heard Moses express his feelings so candidly. It touched her deeply. She walked up to him and gave him a hug.

"Thank you," she said, leaning her head on his shoulder. And once again, there was not a hint of her habitual foolishness.

Moses did not know if the hug meant that she was going to stay; he did not want to know just yet. It was just good to have her there. So they worked together quietly on fixing dinner, ate in relative silence, and then sat together in the yard, after the sun had gone down, just looking at the stars.

"Do you believe in God?" Rosy asked, when they had not said anything for quite some time. It was a deep question coming, as it was, from a twelve-year-old. Throughout the conversation that followed, she never laughed once.

"Yeah, sure," Moses said. "Why?"

"Does he talk to you?"

"Talk to me? Of course not! I just believe in him; I'm not a prophet or something," Moses retorted.

"Do you talk to *him*, then? Do you ask him what he wants you to do?"

"If I can't hear him, how can he tell me what he wants me to do?" Moses laughed. "Rosy, I just try to be nice to people, that's all."

"Everybody likes you," Rosy said.

"Right, and if you're nice to people, they'll like you too," said the big brother. "It's the best way to get ahead. It worked for me... in America, and in my business."

After a long silence, Rosy asked, "But what about God? Don't you try to be nice to people for him?"

"No, I do it for myself, Rosy. If you don't take care of yourself, no one else will."

Another pause. Then Rosy said, "God talks to *me*."

"Wah!" Moses turned around to face his sister as he asked her quite earnestly "What does he say?"

"Not like a voice, but like in my heart," she said. "Like I know I have to do something." Disappointment showed on Moses' face, as Rosy went on: "I know I have to go with Winky. He wants me there. It's about something big that is going to happen."

"Are we going to go back over that?" Moses asked angrily.

Rosy did not answer. And Moses did not say anything more.

An hour later, Rosy went to the mattress on her side of the hut, lay herself down, and fell asleep.

The next morning, when Moses got up he noticed that his sister's bed was empty. *She must be working in the shamba*, he thought. But when he went out in the yard there was no sign of her.

He raced back into the hut, pulled a box out from under her side of the couch, where Rosy kept her clothes, and it was empty.

Chapter 15--Destruction

Moses never fully recovered from Rosy leaving him. In some ways it was harder than the loss of his parents. But his special ability to direct attention away from personal pain was enough to carry him through. He tried to look on the positive side: There was nothing stopping him from visiting Rosy, and now there was time to make friends with the other *boda-boda* drivers.

In the end, however, his resolve not to drink, and the extra demands of doing Rosy's work in the *shamba* did not allow for much time with anyone apart from his best friend, Jiddy. His left arm had become so strong that he had little difficulty swinging the *jembe*, and he even learned how to do a reasonable job of laying bricks, with Jiddy's help. They were making plans for Jiddy to move in with him when the house was finished.

Then, in May of that same year, when Moses was still only fifteen years old, something happened which shook the entire world. It was not the immediate sensation in Shinyalu, tucked away in the Kenyan interior, that it was in the rest of the world, but Kenyans did have radio contact, and word of mouth travelled almost as quickly.

Something terrible had happened in America. The whole country had been attacked in a huge air strike... practically blown off the map. Millions of people were dead, and those who were still alive were fleeing the country to escape radiation, disease, and starvation. It was the biggest loss of human life in the history of the world.

Moses tried to text Ray but could not get through. Weeks later, Ray texted him with a new mobile number. He had been out of the country, in England, when the attack took place. Some of his relatives had survived but were stranded in the U.S. Nevertheless, for Moses, even Ray's family and friends were just statistics. Others in the village were even more indifferent to the actual sufferings of people they had never met. It was not so different to how Americans would have felt if they had received word that a village in Kenya had been wiped out.

Moses knew that his friend had bigger worries than sending messages to some teenager in Africa, and so he tried not to text too often; but each time he did, Ray was kind enough to send a short reply. He asked Moses to pray for his family in particular. Ray had never said anything to sound religious before that, but the boy could appreciate that, at a time like this, almost anyone would be praying. It was some weeks later that Ray's family escaped the holocaust and joined him in England.

The fall of America was a turning point in world history. It was understandable that people talked about it constantly. Those who had no radios would crowd around those who did, in order to get the latest updates. And newspapers sold out as quickly as they arrived from Nairobi. But apart from talk, life was surprisingly normal there in the village. People still worked their farms; made the long walk into Kakamega to sell produce, get supplies, or visit the hospital; and they still plied their trades, which, in Moses' case, meant taking customers up and down the dirt road to their various destinations.

One Saturday, two weeks after the attack, Josephat returned. Moses had been off on a fare to Kakamega when the itinerant prophet did his post office talk, but he learned from others that Josephat was claiming that he had predicted the fall of America. People accepted that he had been talking about destruction for "those who had destroyed the earth" before it happened, but most could not agree that he had specifically indicated that it would be America.

Moses was passing Amy's place late that afternoon. He was without a customer, so he decided to pop in and see his sister. Josephat was in the front room with three of the children, who were at a table doing their homework.

"You were right," Josephat said to Moses, when Amy had left to get Rosy from the backyard.

"Right about what?" Moses asked.

"About America being the ones God was going to destroy," Josephat said.

"I didn't say he was going to destroy *anyone*!" Moses said defensively. "And you didn't either."

"But you said Americans were destroying the world, didn't you?" Josephat asked. "And that's the people God said he was going to destroy."

He wants to drag me into his stupid prediction, Moses thought. And he did not want to be a part of it.

Just then Amy came back, and the topic shifted.

"Rosy's just finishing some haircuts," she explained. It seemed to Moses that, in the short time she had been there, Rosy was learning more at Amy's than at school.

Benji had been teaching her how to play the guitar, and Amy had taught her some fancy cooking. Now she was learning how to cut hair, not that it took much skill to shave heads, which was the preferred style for both males and females in rural Kenya. Amy had hand-operated clippers with an attachment that would leave a tiny bit of hair on and still keep it the same length all over the head.

Josephat had offended Moses. He could see that. So when Rosy came in, he left the boy to talk with his sister while he and Amy moved to the other end of the room and spoke quietly with each other. Moses could not resist listening, even when it meant missing some of what Rosy was saying.

"What do you reckon it means for us?" Moses heard Amy ask Josephat quietly.

"I can't truly say," Josephat replied. "He didn't give me any other 'structions. We just hafta be faithful, sister. There's others waiting too."

"Are you listening or not?" Rosy had become an avid talker since moving in with Amy, and she wanted a listener. Moses was happy to see the change in her.

"Sorry, Rosy," he said. "The haircuts... yeah. Is this the first time you've done it?"

"Today, yeah. Anna showed with the first one, and then I did it by my own. The little kids cry and fuss, but Anna helped to hold them steady."

Then she shifted the focus. "How is the house?"

"We're getting there. Jiddy's parents are helping with bricks, because he's going to stay with me."

"First they give him that bike, and now this," Rosy answered. "They think he is a baby."

"I won't complain," Moses laughed.

Jiddy's parents were wealthier than most in the village, and so, when he had done poorly at school, they had decided to give him a head start as a *boda-boda* driver by getting him the best bike in the village. At least it had been the best until Moses had arrived with his.

*   *   *

Over the next year and a half, the house was built to the point where Jiddy could move in. Life in general improved in Shinyalu, and in much of Kenya.

The fall of America was, indeed, a horrible tragedy, but the fallout had been mostly good for the Kenyan economy. The whole world was taking in American refugees, and benefiting from it. More than twenty thousand had been brought to Kenya, and their professional skills contributed to the economy without draining excessive profits away, as had happened in the past.

The United Nations was taking responsibility for rebuilding the economy. The dynamic leader of this new world order was U:N. Secretary General Xu Dangchao. The power vacuum left by the fall of America gave Dangchao opportunities that no previous Secretary General had ever come close to experiencing. He was able to use his powers to both entice and punish various national governments, and he seemed to be using this strategy for the good of everyone. Kenya was one of many countries that benefited from it.

Government workers were getting better salaries now in exchange for restraints on bribes and other forms of corruption. Even the police roadblocks, which had been used in the past to extort bribes from *matatu* and truck drivers, gradually disappeared. The Kenyan Government was able to exercise greater control over foreign investments, and U.N. intervention (especially restrictions on foreign trade) was ensuring that the benefits gained through those investments reached the masses in a way that they never had before. Tea plantations were being ripped out and other crops planted in their place. This led to price drops for maize and other staples.

"Whatever it is, I like it, Stump," Jiddy said to Moses early one morning when they were planting beans together on the *shamba*, before heading off to work. Moses who was seventeen by this time, had to explain a lot of things to the youth, who was his senior by almost three years. Perhaps it was because of his low self esteem that Jiddy took to calling Moses "Stump", reminding his friend of his missing right forearm. When he first started doing it, Moses was too taken up with the privilege of having an older friend to think of complaining, and even though he said enough to let Jiddy know that it bothered him now, Jiddy persisted with the habit that had built up over the past three years.

"It's because people are sharing things more equally now," Moses explained. "It's bringing prices down. America used to waste everything when it wasn't their land that was being used. Now we have enough for everyone in Kenya, as long as we don't waste.

"*Waste not, want not,* Jiddy. That's what Winky taught me when I first started working."

"Waste not, want not," Jiddy repeated as he struggled to understand what it meant. "Thanks, Stump."

Moses had passed other wisdom on to Jiddy in the course of their friendship, and some of it was sinking in, especially now that they were living together. Jiddy was being more careful with his finances now, and it had helped him to achieve a modicum of business success. He had managed to save up enough (along with some help from his parents) to become the second *boda-boda* driver in Shinyalu to get a scanner phone. And this had led to even more benefits, because more and more people were getting the microchip implant now. It was truly the way of the future for both of them.

Chapter 16--God's Good Earth

"I'm getting one in Kakamega tomorrow," Jiddy announced one Sunday afternoon in May of Moses' seventeenth year.

They were talking about the microchip implant that had brought them both so much business over the past year. "Hey, Stump, why don't you get one too?"

With financial help from Jiddy's parents, they had finished the house well ahead of Moses' original target date, and they had been sharing it together for almost a year now.

Moses could see the good sense in what Jiddy was saying. There was an implant available which could be put on the forehead of anyone who did not have a right hand. Having his own implant would mean the bank could more or less do his books for him, giving him more time to stay ahead of the other *boda-boda* drivers. Government subsidies had made it possible for almost any business to get a scanner now, and implants were free. In the past month, three other *boda-boda* drivers had purchased scanner phones. As a result, Moses and Jiddy had lost some of their old customers.

"I don't know," Moses said. "I kind of promised Winky I wouldn't."

But it wasn't just Winky pushing Moses not to get an implant. He often shared his thoughts with Ray via text message, and he had been surprised when, in a recent exchange, Ray had said something that sounded a lot like Winky. In fact, it was even more like Josephat.

"Don't take it, Mo," Ray had typed into the handset. "Believe me, it will bring big problems."

Now what could Ray have been talking about? Ray had been a supporter of banks when they first met in Chicago three years earlier, although he had shared some thoughts about economics and life since then, which struck Moses as being a bit more radical.

"U said it urself: money won't fix things," Ray had reminded him in one text message. "Americans learned 2 late. Greed was our downfall." He said things against banks too, warning Moses not to trust them. It was so different from the man Moses had met in Chicago.

Moses did not get an implant with Jiddy, but he had a feeling that he would eventually. His dislike for Josephat was destined to overcome his respect for Amy and Ray.

Since January, Josephat had been turning up more often, accompanied by someone different each time. Together they would put up posters about his theories. He was doing something funny with Amy, and even with Rosy. Rosy had become Amy's main helper after Benji got a job in Nairobi with a trucking company, and after Anna moved in as housekeeper for a family in Kakamega. Amy still had the seven youngest children; so Rosy, now 14, dropped out of school to help fulltime.

Kyme stopped sending funds shortly after the fall of America. He apologised, and begged her to forgive him for it, but gave no reason, and neither Moses nor Amy questioned him further about it. Amy ended up selling the Hi-Ace and economsing in other ways to stretch the funds he had sent over almost two years.

One Saturday in June, just after Rosy had turned fifteen, Moses came to see Amy, and was surprised to find the house empty, apart from the old Aboriginal woman and four-year-old Karla.

"Where is everyone, Winky?" Moses asked cheerfully.

"They went with Josephat," she answered. "They're out exploring."

Moses scowled and said nothing. He had a right to complain about his sister being pulled into this, didn't he? She was his sister, after all, and she had only just turned fifteen. He decided to ask a few more questions first.

"Exploring what?" he asked.

"Exploring God's good earth," she answered.

"Yeah, but what part of it?"

"Now what difference could that make to you, boy?" Amy asked as she leaned forward where she sat, with both hands on her knees.

Moses had no answer for that, but he knew Amy was hiding something.

"I don't like Rosy being around him," he said after a short pause. "He's a *'nipulator*, that's what he is."

"Moses, he's a good man," she vouched. "And Rosy likes him. True."

"Well, I don't!" Moses snapped back. "And I say she should stay away from him."

Amy thought for a while before answering. "I'm sad to hear that, boy. You talk to Rosy about it when she gets back, ay?"

"And when will that be?" he asked.

"Tomorrow sometime."

"Tomorrow? Where are they going to stay tonight? And who's going to look out for Rosy?"

"Josephat is with them," Amy replied sweetly. "He and Rosy can take care of themselves; and, Moses, you must know the good Lord is there with them too." The tiniest twitch in Winky's eye did not go unnoticed by Moses.

Josephat was the one Moses wanted his sister protected *from*. And he hardly thought the good Lord would interfere if the man got some crazy notion to molest her. He was secretly determined to return the next day so that he could be waiting for Rosy... and Josephat... when they returned.

*   *   *

Shortly after the sun came up the next morning, Moses was biking down to Amy's house, so he would be there in plenty of time. He was surprised to see two of the children out playing in the yard.

"Is Rosy back?" he asked Jo-Jo, who was now seven years old.

"Eh," said Jo-Jo, nodding his head as he concentrated on throwing a ball in the air and catching it.

"When did you get back?"

"Last night," Jo-Jo said.

"Where did you go?"

"Exploring God's good earth," the boy replied, obviously echoing something that he and Amy had both been told to say.

Moses was seriously thinking of threatening the boy to get more information, but just then Rosy walked around the corner of the house.

"Hi, Moses," she said enthusiastically.

Just seeing her, safe and sound, and with such a cheerful outlook, melted Moses' resolve to make a scene. She was unharmed; they had not been out all night after all; and what good reason could he give for trying to tell her who she could or could not associate with? But she was evasive, like the others, about what they had been doing. That continued to bother him.

He voiced his anger with Jiddy that afternoon, as they worked together in front of their new home. It was harvest time and they had maize to be rubbed off the cobs.

Jiddy agreed, as Moses told him for about the hundredth time, that he did not trust Josephat. The more Jiddy heard it, the more he believed it. They both saw evil in almost anything the man did. As the pile of kernels grew on a mat in front of them and a pile of empty cobs grew on either side, their hatred for Josephat grew with it.

"People in the village are too trusting, Stump," Jiddy said. "It's all love, love, love now, with everyone working together. But Obadiah knows something is wrong."

Obadiah, who had been so tolerant of Josephat over the years, and who was spearheading a drive to unite the local churches, was bothered that Josephat (and those who helped him put up posters) was not showing any interest in being a part of it.

"Obadiah said just be patient and wait," Jiddy said. "He knows, but he said we have to be nice, for now."

"I just hope he doesn't wait too long," Moses said.

The whole world had been on a 'nice' drive for the past two years, as they all sought to comfort themselves over what had happened to America.

Josephat had been openly critical of Dangchao, the U.N. General Secretary, at least at the start. He claimed Dangchao was secretly evil, and one day he would die and be resurrected by the devil. This angered Moses and many others, who could see that the preacher was just jealous. The world had never seen such a benevolent leader as Dangchao, and this was a time when they needed the strong uniting force that he offered.

Then Josephat had gone quiet. He had stopped his traditional talks at the post office, choosing to visit people quietly now... Amy in particular... and put up posters. He often arrived in a truck now, laden with printed material that was being circulated wherever they went. And these helpers of his were almost all from other tribes... not Luhyas at all.

But, like Jiddy said, these were times of great tolerance. Tribal tensions had been over-ruled by bigger economic issues, and so it was in everyone's best interests to get along, and to cooperate with the strategies which had helped to bring about so much peace and prosperity. In the light of that, it was a small price to pay, for Moses and Jiddy to hide their dislike for Josephat.

Besides, like Obadiah appeared to be saying, the tolerance was not going to last forever.

Chapter 17--Implanted

Six months after his friend got an implant, and shortly after he turned 18, Moses received another visit from Mr. Barasa, from the micro-bank. This time there was no mention of visiting Amy, as it seemed that the bank manager knew as well as Moses did that she would not approve. He came, instead, to Moses' house on a Sunday afternoon, when he knew Moses would be there.

"So this is the new house!" he exclaimed, as he leaned back with hands on his hips and admired the teenager's work. "And you did all this yourself?"

"No. Jiddy, my friend, helped with some of it," he said. Actually, Jiddy had done at least half of the work, but he was not there, and Moses did not mind taking a little more than his share of the credit for the construction.

"We're going to put glass in the windows next week," he announced proudly. "Then we can start saving for furniture."

"So your business is going well?" Barasa asked. In fact, he had made a few enquiries, and he knew as well as Moses how things were going.

"I am having a little recession just now," Moses confessed. "Everyone has scanners these days, and now three other drivers have ten-speeds."

"I have another proposition for you, Moses," the bank manager announced. "I won't guarantee it'll help your business, but you would be paid more than enough to fill your house with the finest furniture, just for taking another trip overseas. What do you think about that?"

"Tell me about it!" Moses said with a huge grin, as he eagerly motioned for Mr. Barasa to take a seat on a bench that leaned against the front of his house. Moses sat himself down on the ground in front of the bench.

"You were a big hit for the micro-bank," Barasa said. "Now some other banks want to use you in a bigger campaign... a promotion for the identification implant."

Moses was not paying much attention. He just wanted to know where they would be sending him. Chicago, of course, had been destroyed two and a half years earlier, and virtually all of the U.S. was uninhabitable now; so it had to be somewhere outside the U.S. "Where will I go?" Moses asked, knowing that he would be happy to go anywhere, just for the excitement of travelling.

"London," Mr. Barasa replied.

Moses' heart leapt. Ray was living in London now. Maybe they could see each other again. Maybe he could even meet Ray's family this time.

"Of course we'll have to arrange an implant for you first," Mr. Barasa said. "We want to give the impression that you have had one all along."

How did Mr. Barasa know that he didn't yet have an implant? He used a different bank now, and he didn't think his bank would have shared such information.

"I'll need pictures of you here in the village before you leave... like last time: on the bike, using the scanner, and," he said, turning around on the bench to crane his neck at the house which was behind him, "working on your house... maybe putting glass in the windows."

Moses was thinking about Winky. What would she think? He would do what was best for himself in the end, of course, but he wanted as little hurt for Amy as possible. It would be impossible to hide the fact that he was going, but maybe he could just make up some other reason.

While this was going on inside his head, he still managed to get details about travel plans, how much they would pay him, what he would have to do, and, of course, how soon he would need to get the implant.

"I can take you back to Kakamega with me right now," Barasa said. "I know a doctor who is open on Sundays. That way you won't miss any time off work tomorrow."

It all seemed so rushed. On the other hand, he had delayed for six months longer than Jiddy already. Sure, why not get it today!

On the drive to Kakamega in Barasa's four-wheel drive, Moses was unusually silent. His heart was racing, and he had broken into a sweat. It had something to do with the implant. Why did he feel so uncomfortable about it? Was it really something unforgiveably evil that he was doing? Surely it was just Winky's talk that had done it. And Ray's. And, most of all, Josephat's.

Mr. Barasa stopped to show off his *shamba* just outside Kakamega. Actually, it was more of a plantation, with hundreds of fruit trees... all purchased from what he had made in the bank. A flock of birds swooped on his trees, and Barasa snatched a shotgun from under a box on the back porch and fired in their direction. It killed a few, but the real purpose was just to scare the others.

"Go and tell your friends about it!" Barasa shouted to the birds, hoping that they would all learn to stay away.

Then they were off to get the implant. Moses hardly felt a thing as the doctor inserted the needle and let the tiny microchip slip from the syringe into the flesh on his forehead. It was so small that he could not even feel it when he ran his fingers over his forehead after leaving the surgery.

That wasn't so bad, he thought as he bounced down the road in a crowded *matatu* on the journey back to Shinyalu. It was like he had expected God to strike him down dead just for getting it, when he could see now that it was really nothing at all.

The next week, filming began. Amy seemed almost distracted from what was happening, and easily accepted his explanation that the bank was just adding to its previous promotions.

A whole team came to organise it all, and they took much longer than the previous cameraman had taken.

Moses was older now, and not as innocent at 18 as he had been at 14, but he could do a few tricks with his bike now, and the film crew spent a long time doing a clip where he appeared to be laying bricks by almost juggling the brick and the trowel with his left hand. It took many takes and a lot of dropped bricks, but they managed to get enough to make it look like he could actually flip a brick in the air and have it land perfectly on the wet cement, with just a tap or two of the trowel to set it in place before more cement would go on top of it. And, of course, it finished with Moses' trademark grin.

They interviewed for some time before they got the line they were waiting for; but it came eventually.

"I was *apprehensible* too … same as others, about getting the implant," he said quite earnestly. "But look at me now? I don't feel a thing." And he dragged his finger across his forehead while smiling widely.

The promotion clip was virtually finished when Moses left for London a few weeks later, but they wanted him to meet the world's media in a place where he would be more accessible. They also added some humorous shots of him doing such things as playing in snow in London, for the first time in his life. He hid the fact that he really hated the stuff. Even with a ton of coats and scarves and gloves, he could not believe that people really lived in such a painfully cold environment.

At least the hotel and other buildings were well heated, so he enjoyed film shoots of him registering amazement at the luxuries available in such shops as Harrods. With assurances from the organisers that they would pay the bill, he ended up buying an elaborately carved small black mahogany coffee table, and grinning for the camera as a scanner was pulled across his forehead to give the impression that he had paid for it himself.

The trip was shorter than he had hoped, but there were a couple of free hours in the middle of the day, just before he was scheduled to fly home, and he had arranged for Ray to meet him in the hotel lobby. Ray came alone.

"Where's your family?" Moses asked when they had shaken left hands.

"They've been very busy, Moses," Ray said. "Actually, my son is in South Africa with another friend of his, and my daughter is in Rome."

"What about your wife?" Moses asked. "Is she in London?"

"Yes she is, and she sends her apologies. Like I said, we've been busy. Irene is entertaining some visitors from overseas at this very moment." Then Ray changed the subject.

"But what about you? What brings you here? Your message said something about the bank."

The meeting was going to be a brief one, and so Moses decided to try what had worked so well with Winky.

"They wanted to do more promotions," he said. "Same as last time."

"The *micro-bank* wanted to do more promotions?" Ray asked suspiciously.

"No, some other banks. It's nothing really."

Ray could tell Moses was hiding something, but he did not probe further.

"How is Rosy?" Ray asked, to change the subject yet again.

"She's living with Winky now, didn't I tell you?"

"Yes, you did. But surely you visit her. And how is Winky too?"

"They're both good." And then Moses decided to open up to his friend a bit more. "But not too good. They go away at times and they don't tell me where."

Ray wrinkled his brow in puzzlement. "That sounds strange," he said. "Do you ask?"

"Yeah, sure. But they just say things like 'exploring God's good earth'. That doesn't tell me anything."

"Is she still seeing that Josephat fellow?" Ray asked.

"Yeah, he goes with them," Moses replied.

Ray thought a moment over what to say, and then said, "I don't think you need to worry about it, Moses. I'm sure God is with them."

It was uncanny. Almost the same words that Amy had used. What was going on? Was Moses just imagining some kind of a conspiracy against himself, with Josephat at the top of it?

Moses enjoyed the luxury of treating Ray to a fancy lunch at the five-star hotel (again, courtesy of the bank) and then he took leave to get ready for the trip home. The visit was nothing like the exciting excursions that Moses had experienced with Kyme, but then his relationship with Ray was different... more intense, even if it *was* restricted to one or two text messages each week.

Moses wished later that he had used the time more productively... to talk freely with Ray about his decision to get an implant. He realised too late that, unlike Amy, Ray would almost certainly see the promotions there in London and discover that he was being used to urge all those other people who suffered from 'apprehensions' to go ahead and get the microchip implant. He just hoped that it would not disappoint Ray as much as he knew it would have disappointed Amy.

Chapter 18--Missing!

There was the flight from London, the train from Nairobi, and the *matatu* from Kisumu before Moses was back in Shinyalu. He spotted Jiddy at the bike stand when he arrived in the early afternoon and asked him for help getting his bag and the coffee table out to the house.

"We can stop off and see Rosy on the way," he said.

"They're gone, Stump," Jiddy declared.

"What do you mean 'gone'?" Moses asked, assuming that the children must be out 'exploring' again.

"Really gone," Jiddy added. "They musta sneaked out in the middle of the night, the day after you left. I went by that morning and no one was there. They're gone ... just like that."

Even with travel time, Moses had only been away for six days. That meant the others had been gone for five. It still seemed a long time for Amy to be away without telling anyone. And why hadn't she said anything to him before he left?

Moses tried not to worry, focussing his mind on work and on final touches to the house; but days passed and still no one returned. Then, about two weeks later, he saw someone putting paint on Amy's house. He rode the bike up into the yard to enquire.

"Hey there! Do you know where Amy is?" he shouted up to the tall thin man on the stepladder.

"Amy Walker? No, can't say that I do," the man called down from his perch. "You know she doesn't live here anymore, don't you?"

"Doesn't live here? No way!" Moses exclaimed. "She has to live here. She has a bunch of kids to take care of. My sister's one of them."

"I'm the new owner," the man said as he descended the steps. "Bought this place nearly a month ago. I paid cash. The papers are in the house."

A month ago? That would have been before Moses left for London. Why hadn't Amy said anything to him about it?

Moses tried to be tactful but firm in questioning the older man. He was shown the bill of sale, and was advised to check with the Lands Department in Kakamega if he wanted further proof. The tall man -- the one who considered himself to be the new owner,-- insisted that he had seen no one answering Josephat's description when dealing with Amy, and he had no idea where she and the children had gone. He had heard about the property the same day Amy had listed it with an agent in Kakamega. The price was so good that he snapped it up immediately. He appeared to be a property speculator, probably put onto the giveaway price by the agent himself.

On checking with local *matatu* drivers, Moses learned that Amy and the children had left before sun-up, the day after he had caught the train to Nairobi. That was the same day Jiddy had noticed them missing. The driver remembered Amy and her brood because they were almost a full load in themselves. He had taken them to the railway station in Kisumu, and had assumed that they were just going on an excursion to Nairobi.

"They were sneaking away all right," Moses said to Jiddy. "The train doesn't leave Kisumu until late in the afternoon. It's the only one out of there each day. They didn't need to be at the station so early. So why were they sneaking off?"

The two young men had no answers. They went to Kisumu, where the station master checked his records and found that he had, indeed, sold tickets for Amy and eight children on the train to Nairobi that same day. No one named Josephat was on the records, and no one matching that description had been seen at the station that day or any other in recent memory.

Despite the lack of evidence, Moses and Jiddy were still convinced that Josephat was involved. Moses reported them missing, but the police could see nothing sinister in a local selling up and moving to Nairobi; so they paid Moses little heed.

But for the next two years, he and Jiddy never stopped talking it up around the village. The fact that Josephat never returned during that time was enough to convince most people that the boys were probably right. But nothing could be done without more evidence.

Had Amy and Rosy been willing victims, or were they under a spell? For his part, Moses was convinced Josephat had been using traditional magic on all of them and had been doing so for quite some time. He believed that it had led to them being lured away, possibly to their deaths.

"They would never have left without telling me," he argued repeatedly.

Chapter 19--Unity

If Moses had ever thought that he could keep his reason for going to London secret, he soon learned otherwise. In a matter of weeks posters started to appear around the village and all over Kakamega with his face on them and the slogan "no more apprehensions" written across it... in English and in Luhya. Those few locals who had televisions were soon spreading the word about Moses' acting abilities too. Everyone loved him, and they told him so. His business picked up dramatically; *everyone* wanted to be seen with the poster boy.

The campaign was working for the banks too, because people all over Western Kenya started queueing to get implants. A monthly mobile clinic visited villages to inject microchips under the skin of the right hand on all those who wished to be a part of the new economy. Newspapers reported similar happenings all over the world.

Incentives were making the transition even easier. Scanners were free to any business that qualified now, and even the churches were being enticed with offers that were just too good to refuse.

Quakers, Pentecostals, and traditional churches were being lured into linking up with Catholics, who were themselves making concessions in order to get the premiums that were being offered by the government in conjunction with a restructured ecumenical super-church.

There had been whispered debates over whether the churches would install scanners, after claims had circulated about the implant being the devil's mark. But the government sidestepped that by promising to eliminate the need for offerings altogether for all who became a part of the new super-church. Any group joining up would be funded at a rate that far exceeded what they were getting through their meager offering plates each Sunday. Funding would be paid electronically into church accounts by the government. Of course most attenders were getting implants anyway, because they needed them to do business; but church subsidies kept the issue from becoming a source of debate on Sunday mornings.

"It's three or four times what we ever got from Friends in America," one young Quaker enthused to the others at the *boda-boda* stand one morning. Quakers in Kenya had previously relied on their wealthier counterparts in America; consequently, after the fall of America, they had been suffering financially. Now all that was changing. "I'm sure the Lord is using this to bless us," said the young Quaker-turned-superchurchman. "There is so much good we can do with this money."

"What about tribal practices? Will they stop us from doing our old family customs?" asked another.

"The church never stopped us from doing circumcisions or other practices, not even before," boasted a driver from a zealous Catholic family. "And there are meetings during the week now where you can believe anything you like. It'll be so easy in this new church."

"What about you, Moses? What's your religion?" asked the Quaker driver.

"Me, I don't have a religion," he said. "Just do good and think positive; that's my religion. But I'm happy for you guys."

Talk then turned to General Secretary Xu Dangchao. There was praise from all of them for the charismatic leader. In less than four years he had turned the greatest holocaust in history into a booming success for those who had survived. World peace, prosperity, and religious unity; they had it all. It was like heaven on earth.

Maybe there was a little truth in what Josephat said, Moses thought to himself. "Those who destroyed the earth" had, themselves, been destroyed, and the rest of the world was reaping great benefits as a result. Too bad that Josephat (and Amy, and Rosy) couldn't see that what Dangchao was building was closer to the paradise that they must have been hoping for, than anything that they had now... if, in fact, they were even alive.

The trouble, he thought, was that Josephat had been a fanatic. He had to believe he was right about *everything*. Josephat had refused to co-operate with other believers, who were uniting under this new enlightened church. His stubbornness had led to insanity. Breakaway groups like his always seemed to turn into cults, with sick beliefs and sicker practices. Each time Moses thought of Rosy, Amy, and Josephat, his anger grew.

As the stories had spread, people came to believe that Amy and the children had been brainwashed, hypnotised, and then enticed away to some secret hideaway, where, if they were still alive, they were almost certainly carrying out satanic rituals and suffering a fate worse than death. Most believed that the orphan family never reached Nairobi on that fateful train trip, before Josephat succeeded in having his way with them.

Over the next two years, while unity spread through churches, through banks, and through governments, there was a subtle growth in suspicion about anyone who refused to be a part of this new movement. Moses had been asked countless times to join the new church himself, but he had always refused, saying that he had no need of such stuff. The simple fact that he hung onto his independence made many people feel that he was against what they were doing. He had to repeatedly defend their right to believe as they did, in order to reassure them.

It seemed like Moses was only able to get away with maintaining ths position because he was in a class of his own, as the worldwide poster boy for the identity system that was uniting the planet. His celebrity status gave him confidence enough to carry on without religious affiliation, even if it did not make him independent in other ways.

There were others like himself, who claimed to believe in nothing, but the counter-argument was always that there was room for those sort of people in the new world church too. Such people usually joined in the end, just for the feeling of acceptance that it gave them. But more than a few joined out of fear that they would suffer by not being a visible supporter of the new movement.

Chapter 20--Becoming a Man

In those first heady days of fame and financial success, Moses found himself the center of attention for a lot of attractive females in the village. Although promiscuity was rampant amongst local youth, Moses had, until he was 18, avoided any sexual relationships for two main reasons. One was his total dedication to becoming successful. Women represented a distraction from his long-term goals of financial independence.

But the other reason was probably more significant, and that was that he had never been circumcised. The loss of his parents had come at a time when most boys his age were beng circumcised to prove their manhood. This lapse on his part had gone completely unnoticed. But a sexual relationship would give a woman information that, if spread around, could lead to him being forcibly circumcised in accordance with local custom. He did not want that. Even married men were, at times, dragged into the bloody ritual if people learned that they had been overlooked in previous years.

Who could say how long his hormonal needs would have held out against his fear of adult circumcision? Nevertheless, Moses had found some comfort in the fact that during this time of greater unity, there had also developed a greater tolerance for non-circumcised males.

When he was nearly 19, Jiddy talked him into sleeping with Atamba, a local woman in her mid twenties who worked in the local bar. Jiddy was the only other person on earth who knew Moses' secret about being uncircumcised, and he had faithfully kept it.

"She won't tell anyone," Jiddy promised. "Atamba knows lots of secrets... about me and about a lot of other guys in the village, but she never tells anything. And hey, Stump, she doesn't cost much either."

The time was past when Moses would need to reckon with tribal elders, even if his secret did leak out, thanks to the new religious liberalism. So Moses let Jiddy introduce him to this woman, and he lost his virginity on the floor of Atamba's hut on the opposite side of the village to where he lived, very late one night after the bar closed. Not feeling right about paying for such a favour, he gave her two kilograms of sugar "as a gift" instead, and she seemed happy with that.

"Now you're a man," Jiddy had said the next morning, after Moses timidly let him know that he had "done it". "What do you think, Stump? Was it good?"

"It was okay," he said sheepishly, "but I was worried about someone finding us. Do all the girls do it?"

"Most, if you're nice to them," Jiddy promised. He was pretending to be more expert than he really was, although he *had* enjoyed the company of three or four local women in the five years that had passed since his first encounter at the age of 16.

The experience had opened Moses' eyes to what he had been missing, and so after that, he frequently obliged various women who threw themselves at him because of his fame. But he always practiced safe sex (unlike some others in the village), and he did not let it interfere with his greater desire to succeed financially.

Jiddy benefited from his friendship with Moses, often inheriting a friend of someone whom Moses was bringing back to the house. He did not have the same dedication to his job that Moses had, so he was not worried about taking time off work during the day to engage in sex.

Girls lost interest in Jiddy much more quickly than they did with Moses, but the younger man was always able to use his fame to find Jiddy a new playmate.

"Be nice to them. You said it yourself," Moses lectured one night after seeing his friend's latest girlfriend storm out of the house as he was cycling up to it. "What do you do to make them so mad? She looked like she had been hit."

"They don't know what they want," Jiddy grizzled. "Even they like it rough too sometimes, but then they change when I'm having fun."

Just as Moses had suspected. Jiddy was hitting them and getting turned on by it. No wonder the girls left him after a few dates! He tried reasoning with Jiddy, explaining that his own approach was more successful.

"Yeah, *you* can say that, Stump," Jiddy argued, "because you're famous. But I know better than you, because I've had a lot more girls."

Moses did not bother to say the obvious. There was no point in rubbing Jiddy's nose in his numerous failures. Instead, Moses resolved to look for ways to subtly influence his friend. What would often happen is that the girls Jiddy upset came to Moses for comfort. He had strict rules about not taking advantage of any of them, however. He valued Jiddy's friendship too much to do that.

Chapter 21--Josephat Spotted

Moses never gave up looking for Rosy, Amy, and the children, but all of his efforts were fruitless. He had travelled to Nairobi and made enquiries there twice, once shortly after they disappeared, and again a year later. He hired a private investigator to search for them, but there were no records of the children in any of the schools, and the only Amy Walkers found in document searches all turned out to be someone else. Josephat, too, had not been seen, either locally or in Nairobi. It was like they had all disappeared off the face of the earth.

Locals were easily convinced that Amy and the children had been killed, and that Josephat had fled to another country; whereas Moses was not so quick to write them off completely.

Then, two months after he turned 20, in early February, there was a report that someone matching Josephat's description had traded a box full of used postage stamps for some pain killers at a chemist shop in Kakamega. Attempts to trace where he had come from, or where he had gone afterwards led nowhere; but it was enough to convince Moses that Rosy and the others were still alive, and that they had returned to the area from Nairobi. The stamps must have been the same ones that he himself had donated to Amy when she was still living in the village. Moses made this known to others in Shinyalu, and, because it was widely believed by now that the family had been killed, this even aroused the interest of the local police, who started making enquiries of their own, both in Shinyalu and in Kakamega.

Talk of drinking blood and worshipping devils resumed, as well as theories about the children being abused, tortured, and killed. People became convinced that others in Kakamega were conspiring to hide and protect Josephat. One of the people fruitlessly interviewed by the police, lived on the road between Shinyalu and Kakamega, and so a group of *boda-boda* drivers decided to surround the man's house and set fire to it, as punishment for supposedly withholding information.

Moses protested weakly, stating that they did not have enough evidence to act, but their anger over-ruled. Luhya teaching is that if you kill anyone, the ghost will return to haunt you. Even burning someone's home is considered taboo; but all that was changing now. Moses felt obliged to pedal with the brigade to the man's house, but he refrained from actually starting the fire. The victim's wife and daughter escaped into a field (He himself was at work in town.), but all that they owned went up in smoke.

The simmering hatred that people felt toward Josephat for having spoken out against the new government, and against the implant, was threatening to boil over in other ways as well. It was getting harder and harder for people like Obadiah to maintain the veneer of tolerance that had been a part of the superchurch platform. There was, indeed, plenty of tolerance within the new structure, but those who teach tolerance most loudly often become themselves the most intolerant toward people outside their control. This powerful new association had equally powerful negative feelings toward dissidents. Such "incompatibility" was quickly becoming the ultimate sin.

In Shinyalu, Josephat symbolised all who dared to question the way the world was going. There was an almost utopian paradise forming on one hand, and deep insecurity on the other. Hate for Josephat became the focus that helped many to overcome their insecurities.

Then, five months after the stamps turned up in Kakamega, tragedy struck. Secretary General Xu Dangchao, the architect of the new world order, had been attacked and killed during an appearance in Jerusalem. A crazed assassin had shot him in the head and in the heart, before being killed himself. Dangchao had died on the way to hospital. The world was in shock, as people realised how much they had depended on Dangchao to turn the economy around. Now he was gone.

In the midst of the shock, Moses recalled something that Josephat had said almost exactly three years earlier. He had said that Dangchao was going to die, and that Satan was going to resurrect him. It was like the fall of America; but this time he had named Dangchao. Moses didn't care if it was Satan or not; he still wished for a miracle... something to bring back the man who had almost single-handedly made poverty a thing of the past.

Then, the next day, it *did* happen. News came via radio first, with further reports in the papers: Dangchao was alive. They said earlier reports had been a mistake; but over the next three years Dangchao often reminded the world of his 'miraculous resurrection' whenever there were doubts about his authority. Miracle or not, he had survived, with nothing to show for it but a patch over one eye, where a bullet had entered his skull.

There were wild celebrations organised by the new world church. They were held in the village, in Kakamega, in Nairobi, in fact, all over the world when the news of Dangchao's survival reached the masses. In the minds of everyone, Dangchao had been dead, and now he was alive. He had become a living legend... a god.

But the assassination attempt was a warning to the world. They needed to take better care of their gifted leader. The Jews had put up a new Temple in Jerusalem some three years earlier, and it had come to symbolise the new era of peace, prosperity and religious harmony that Dangchao had been so instrumental in bringing about. The Jews graciously agreed to offer use of their Temple as Dangchao's official headquarters (although there were rumours that not all Jews had been so gracious about the offer).

Some people saw deep significance in what was happening in Jerusalem, including a few of the on-going independent believers in the village; but all Moses cared about was that the world was safe... and so was its charismatic leader. He felt proud to have played his part in easing the transition from one economy to another through the advertising campaign for the microchip implant, and so he identified strongly with this new world that had grown out of the destruction of "those who had destroyed the earth".

So what, if Josephat had said that Satan would be the force to bring Dangchao back from the dead! The important thing was that he had come back, and that steps were being taken to make sure that it stayed that way.

Chapter 22--Amy and the Kids

"What have you got there?" Amy asked, as Karla neared the summit of the steep hill, hugging an armload of vegetables. The youngest member of the family, now seven years old, had been out harvesting from secret locations scattered around the Kakamega Forest.

"Sweet potatoes," she said. "Jo-Jo has some honey." Ten-year-old Jo-Jo was just coming out of the forest at the base of the hill. He waved his arm in a wide circle above his head, a signal Amy recognised immediately. She gathered her few belongings and called to Karla.

"Inside," was all that she said. Karla glanced briefly back at Jo-Jo, who was climbing the hill in earnest now, before she stepped quickly into the manmade cave. She and Amy moved quietly but unhesitantly toward the chamber that was almost fifty metres into the side of the hill. They instinctively protected their faces from the bats that they knew would be at the twenty metre mark.

Meanwhile, ten-year-old Jo-Jo had been joined halfway up the fifty-metre hill by Simon, who, at 12, was the next oldest of the eight children still in Amy's care. Simon had been able to hide the pumpkin he had been carrying under a bush, so he could give Jo-Jo a hand. Together the two were able to carry the bucket of honey more quickly up the hill. Each held one end of a branch extending through the handle of the bucket. It would not do to leave the vessel out where it could be found.

Each person knew what they were to do, and they each acted without saying a word.

When Amy reached the heavy curtain at the back of the cave, which soaked up most of the light from a lantern that burned behind it, she passed the palm of her hand across her face, and 14-year-old Lucy, who had been studying some books, immediately knew that she must blow out the lantern. The pitch blackness was not a handicap to any of them, for they had each learned over the past two years how to navigate every inch of the cave in total silence and without visual assistance.

The tunnel like cave had been constructed by a mining company many years earlier and had been abandoned shortly after its construction. From the tunnel entrance one could look out over the top of the forest, and either see or hear if anyone was in the area. Because the children had been down below gathering food, they had heard something before Amy did, so she knew they all had plenty of time. There was no sense of panic.

When the two boys arrived at the darkened inner chamber, they placed the bucket of honey to the side of the opening and joined the others on a long couch constructed of boxes that were full of pamphlets.

Everything was relaxed as they waited silently for sufficient time to pass. But then they heard a noise at the mouth of the cave. It sounded like several people were entering the cave. Everyone stiffened.

But then there were three loud claps, and they each breathed a sigh of relief. Lucy struck a match and relit the lantern while the others got up and walked toward the opening.

"Jambo!" said the voice of a young woman.

"Rosy!" Karla whispered loudly as she looked up at Amy in the near darkness of the tunnel.

"Eh, Rosy," Amy responded softly, squeezing the little girl's hand. They never shouted, even when they believed the forest to be empty.

"Jambo!" Amy spoke in response to the 17-year-old.

"Look! Micah!" Karla said, as they neared Rosy. "And Jane!" Karla let go of Amy's hand and raced toward the others. Jane's 16-year-old twin brother, Gene, was there too, hidden behind 18-year-old Micah. At 17, Rosy was not the oldest, but she was the natural leader.

For more than two years the family had lived undisturbed in the cave. Tourists never came to the forest at night, nor did they carry pocket lights with them during the day. Any who reached the hill, separated from the dirt track by half a mile of forest, and who ventured into the mouth of the cave, using only matches, soon turned around when they reached the bats. Amy and the children had come to appreciate the bats, who fed on mosquitoes, deterred visitors, and provided them with protein.

"The road was empty, so we jumped out and ran into the forest without anyone seeing," Rosy explained. "I hope we didn't scare you. The truck will be back tonight for more pamphlets. Then they'll be off to Uganda."

It was the sound of the truck stopping that had alerted Jo-Jo and Simon. Normally the older children would arrive and leave late at night, under cover of darkness, so that no one could witness their movements.

The family had been hiding in the forest ever since that day two and a half years earlier, when they had created a false trail that led Moses and others to believe they had gone to Nairobi. It was a simple enough task for Josephat to guide them back, in the middle of the night, to where they had previously spent time exploring "God's good earth".

Over those years, the four older children had often left Amy with the three youngest ones, so that they could assist Josephat and other members of the secret underground movement in northern Kenya and Uganda. Because of their youth, Amy's teens were able to wander freely through the streets of various villages, without arousing suspicion. They would surreptitiously visit members of the movement, often leaving pamphlets and posters to be further distributed by the ones they visited. Josephat was responsible for about 1,000 members of this movement, but there were more than 10,000 others in an area overseen by two leaders in Turkey.

Back in the interior cavern, Amy added a bit more avocado oil to the lantern. They squeezed the oil themselves, from the big green vegetables that grew wild and in abundance in that part of Kenya. Josephat had a secret beehive in the forest, from which they were able to get honey. They used the beeswax to make candles. On the floor of the jungle there were inconspicuous crops of everything from passionfruit and tapioca to guava, pumpkins and wild spinach. Even if someone stumbled onto some of these plants, they just marvelled that they had started growing "wild" in the lush conditions.

Monkeys were a constant threat to anything edible, but root vegetables and the very hard jack fruit always survived in sufficient quantities to keep the family fed, as well as feeding teams that passed through.

During their first year they had raised rabbits high up in the rocks, and used the skins to make blankets, rugs, and even clothes; but it was considered too risky to continue raising them, after a tourist almost discovered one of the hutches. Now they had to rely on more exotic sources of meat.

"Micah, do you feel up to checking the traps?" Amy asked when they had eaten their fill of a hastily prepared lunch, and after they had caught up with the highlights of the latest outing. "We have plenty of time to make stew before the others get here, but I need some meat."

"Can Gene come with me?" Micah asked, looking at Gene to see if he was in favour of it.

"Of course," Amy said, and Gene showed his enthusiasm by leaping up off a box of pamphlets to join Micah on the walk out through the tunnel.

The children all knew how to set string traps for wild birds and moles, which, along with the bats, added flavour to Amy's famous stews.

There was very little that these cave-dwellers needed money for. The last time any of them had gone shopping was when Lucy broke her arm quite badly falling from a tree five months previously. Josephat had taken the last of the stamps that Moses had donated years earlier, and had traded them in Kakamega for pain killers. He knew it was risky, but he could not stand to see her suffer.

Just after Micah and Gene left to check the traps, the other children decided to go outside and scatter themselves around the cave's entrance, where they talked quietly with each other about all that had been happening in Uganda and elsewhere. They always tried to keep someone posted at the entrance, to alert the others if they noted any movment in the forest.

Amy and Rosy stayed back in the chamber to talk.

"Meshach thinks he saw Moses on the road between Shinyalu and Kakamega this morning," Rosy said. "I had to keep down, but I wanted to look so bad."

"Do you miss him much?" Amy asked.

"Course," said Rosy. "He's my brother. But he made his choice, didn't he?"

"Mmm, he did, girl," Amy said sadly. "But It don't make the pain go, does it?"

Rosy just nodded her head, said nothing for a while, and then changed the subject. She had her brother's talent for not dwelling on the negative.

Very late that night, Josephat returned with an older member of the underground movement. The boys had moved boxes of posters down closer to the dirt track as soon as it was dark, so they could load them into the truck quickly before anyone spotted it parked on the road. Fortunately, almost no one ventured into the forest in the middle of the night, for fear of leopards.

Amy had a full hour with Josephat, catching up on news. When he left, he took Rosy and the twins, leaving Micah to help Amy till he returned in two weeks' time.

Chapter 23--Abundance

From the moment that Dangchao returned to office, after the shooting, his approach to government seemed to change. People in Shinyalu did not take much notice at first. In Jerusalem there were wild parties for dignitaries and strange press conferences right from day one, but the changes which affected the masses of the world were more subtle.

Restrictions on factories, mining, exploration, logging, in fact, on anything of environmental concern, just seemed to disappear overnight. It was like hundreds of emissaries had sneaked into the homes of powerful officials all over the world and had whispered thoughts into their heads as they slept... thoughts that would change their entire outlook the next day. They did not even need to wait for approval; they somehow knew that there would be no problem if they chose, from now on, to ignore the rules for the sake of increased production once again.

It would be years before the masses would become aware of what was happening, but in the meantime people were just just too busy rushing to participate in the business boom and too excited revelling in even greater wealth, to be bothered. Investors were making money faster than they could count it; shops were filled to overflowing, and, most importantly, everyone had enough money to buy far more than they needed. The extravagant parties in the former Temple in Jerusalem epitomised the mood of the whole world. Millions... maybe even billions... who had never known much more than a meager existence, were now experiencing the kind of obscene wealth that had led to America's downfall.

It had an effect on the moral fibre of the world too. People wanted more and more indulgent ways to spend their money. Those who were not addicted to wealth as an end in itself would find themselves with more leisure time, to be filled with shopping, being entertained, travelling, eating, and engaging in every form of sexual pleasure that they could imagine.

Some industries, like the travel industry were struggling to keep up with the demand. It took time to build two, three, or four times as many planes, buses, and cars to carry everyone who wanted to use them; but for those who were prepared to pay the increased prices, labour and resources could still be found to create and produce, almost miraculously, all that they wished for. The gods of science and technology were working overtime to feed an insatiable appetite for more and more.

Moses was swept up in all of this too. As had always been his way, he looked ahead, far ahead of his peers. He sold his bike, mortgaged his house, and bought a beautiful new super deluxe Toyota Coaster bus with power steering and an automatic transmission. It had a bigger engine and smoother suspension than any of the other matatus in Shinyalu, plus air-conditioning, and a top quality music system to soothe his passengers on their journeys. People had so much money that he could charge twice what the other drivers were charging and still get passengers, because he gave them each plenty of room in luxurious seats.

The Kakamega road was being sealed too, making the ride even more pleasant for his pampered customers.

Moses had only been working six months when he felt confident enough to buy another Coaster and he hired Jiddy to drive it. Each day, one of them would do the Kakamega run and the other would do the Kisumu run. Each evening they would meet back at the house where Moses would count the takings while Jiddy headed into the village to spend as much of his wealth as he could before getting some sleep and starting another day.

Moses found *his* pleasure by making plans... plans for when he would have a *fleet* of buses to cover the entire area. It never bothered Jiddy that Moses made more than him. After all, he himself was getting many times more than he had ever received while pedalling a bicycle, and he hardly had to move a muscle to do it. It was a dream come true for this unambitious young man.

The village itself was transformed too. Where once there had been street stalls selling tiny piles of vegetables, plastic bowls, and second-hand clothing, now there were air-conditioned shops going up, with rows and rows of shelves full of things to choose from. Electricity had only become affordable during the first three years of Dangchao's reign, but now it was commonplace for homes to have refrigerators, colour TVs, automatic washing machines, and a host of other electrical appliances.

The markets had been extended to include two movie theaters, the busiest one showing nothing but adult movies around the clock. Atamba, the woman who had introduced Moses to sex, now had her own brothel, and the prices were no longer cheap. Dozens of local girls were finding their fortunes by working in it.

People's taste for alcohol had become more sophisticated by this time too. The locally and illegally brewed *chang'aa* was being replaced by imported wines and spirits. To help meet the demand, some maize fields were being turned into grape vineyards. On top of that, more of the Kakamega Forest was being cleared to make room for crops which would provide badly needed bio-fuels.

In the middle of this most exciting time in human history, there was news of a seditious movement out to destroy all that had been so carefully and wisely established. There were two fanatics who were using the internet to preach a message of fear and deception aimed at destroying the government. Official news reports said that they possessed paranormal powers. There was even talk of them being from another world. Their goal was to destroy modern civilisation by first convincing people that Dangchao was evil, and then by getting people to desert him and to drop out of the whole amazing economic utopia.

Alien or not, Moses became convinced that Josephat himself was one of those two men. There were no names and no photos to help people identify them or where they were speaking from, but millions visited their website to hear for themselves the wild ravings.

Moses had his own computer now, and so he occasionally browsed through the site, mostly hoping that it would give a clue as to Josephat's whereabouts. The man obviously had super-human abilities, because news reports said that the posters which had appeared on trees and sign posts all over Kakamega even before Amy moved out, had appeared all over the rest of the world as well.

While Josephat had once been allowed to openly preach and to circulate his crazy ideas, loyal followers of the new world order were now being urged to report anyone seen putting the posters up, or anyone suspected of having connections with the movement. The mood had dramatically changed. Justice was to be swift and harsh for any who supported the underground movement, in order to protect the growing economy from the treacherous lies of the aliens. Anyone found to be supporting the aliens was to be executed.

At first there were rushed attempts at holding trials, but that slowed down the move to stop this insidious influence, and so executions were soon being carried out under direct orders from the various District Officers. There were several from Shinyalu who had been executed, and many more from Kakamega. Moses knew one of the women who was killed, and he was surprised to learn that she had been so foolish as to have fallen for Josephat's lies.

What was becoming clear to him was that even if Amy and the kids were alive, and even if he were to succeed in finding them, unless they dissociated themselves from Josephat and his teachings, they too would face death. The government needed to deal firmly with the threat, but Moses could not bring himself to wish death on Amy and the children. He hated Josephat all the more for the moral dilemma that this had created for him. There must be some way to locate this sub-human, super-human, alien, heretical, kidnapping, false prophet monster, without betraying Amy, Rosy, or any of the others.

Chapter 24--Going Too Far

"What happened to you?" Moses exclaimed as Jiddy came into the house quite late one Friday night after his usual trip to the markets. Jiddy was covered with blood; and Moses jumped up from his desk to assist; but Jiddy smiled broadly on hearing Moses' question.

"I'm okay," he said. "I'm okay. We had another celebration. It was my turn."

"Your turn to do what?" asked Moses. "You're covered in blood!"

"Don't worry, Stump. It's not mine," Jiddy reassured him, as though that was all the explanation that the younger man would need.

"But whose is it?" Moses asked.

"You remember Dinah?" he asked. "The girl you introduced me to at the bullfight a couple years ago, when we were still working as *boda-bodas*?"

Moses remembered the girl. She had suffered some kind of brain damage, but was quite beautiful nonetheless; and she had a gentle, sweet personality.

"We sacrificed her tonight," Jiddy said. "I was the executioner."

"You what?" Moses put his left hand over his face and sat back down in horror.

"Where have you been, Stump?" Jiddy asked. "We've been doing it for months... in the theater... every Friday night. Dinah had something wrong with her anyway. She didn't even know it was going to be her."

"No, no!" Moses shook his head with his hand over his left ear. He did not want to hear any more. "What is happening to us?" he asked, knowing that he would not get a satisfactory answer from his older friend.

"You wanna be careful talking like that," Jiddy said. "We do it for Dangchao. You should see the films they show of people doing it for him in Jerusalem. It kind of cleans out all of the evil in you if you just pour it all into the sacrifice. Everybody feels better afterwards."

Moses still wasn't listening.

"Jiddy, something is very very wrong about this. The whole village is going crazy."

Jiddy suddenly turned deadly serious. "Stump, you gotta watch that," he said. "I mean it. People are dying for saying less than that. I'm your friend and I won't tell, but others would, straight as a spear."

The full impact of what Jiddy had said was sinking in. Moses had been so busy making money that he had not paid much attention to what had been happening over the past year. It was just one more illustration of his ability to focus. He had shut out talk of strange meetings at the superchurch, since he never attended anyway, and he had only been to a couple of the adult shows, preferring to patronise the other theater on those few occasions when he had time for entertainment. Friday nights were so crowded that he had never even tried to attend then.

Jiddy could see that his friend had been shocked, and he tried to comfort him.

"It's happening everywhere, Stump," he said. "Think of it like war. We don't have wars now, so we can afford a few people... just for fun."

Moses shook his head again and stood up to walk outside. *Fun* Jiddy had called it! He had to get away from Jiddy's disgusting justification for such a perverted form of entertainment in a society which had lost all sense of reason and morality.

Out in the open air, Moses looked up at the stars and remembered that night so long ago now, when he and Rosy had looked at the stars. She had been only 12 years old then, and now she would be 18, if she was still alive.

"Do you believe in God?" she had asked. And from that she had moved to asking him if he ever talked to God... or if God had ever talked to him.

He looked up and clenched his one fist. Was it rage? Not really. How could he be angry with a God whom he had never known? But he was struggling with inner turmoil. When he lost his arm, he never blamed anyone, and so why should he blame anyone for what was happening now? But still, something was not right in the village, and maybe in the whole world. Something inside of him cried out for an explanation. Was Dangchao really evil, like Amy and Josephat had said? If Dangchao was behind what was happening in the village, how could he be anything else *but* evil? And the bigger question was, what could he, a struggling small-time businessman living in the Kenyan interior, do about it?

Moses had always concentrated on just looking out for himself, and not bothering with other people's problems. But now he could not bring himself to think about Dinah without feeling revulsion... for Jiddy... for the people in the village... and maybe even for Dangchao.

Economically, things had continued to go well, both for Moses and for the rest of the world. He was close to being able to add another vehicle to his fleet, maybe something bigger this time, that could make a run to and from Nairobi. But he could see that he was being drawn into the very sins that he had condemned the U.S. for six years earlier. People wanted luxury coaches, and the one Moses had his eye on used incredible amounts of fuel. But it had the power and the added features that would pay for itself with satisfied customers.

Perhaps that was what Dangchao was doing too. Maybe he was just trying to keep his "customers" satisfied. *People are so crazy*, Moses thought to himself, still gazing at the stars. He was honest enough to include himself in his observations.

We all want more, even when we don't need it. Unless we have more than everyone else, we're not happy, he thought. For Jiddy the overdose had been pleasure. He had reached a point where he now only found pleasure in seeing someone else suffer. And it appeared that Moses' room mate had a lot of company... both in Shinyalu, and in the greater world outside of their village.

But poor Dinah! And how many others had they treated in the same way?

Chapter 25--Another Disaster

Over the next few weeks, Moses found that, despite all of his previous successes in filtering out the negatives, what Jiddy had done to Dinah rarely left his mind. He knew that his friend was just one of millions who had let themselves become corrupted by whatever was happening to the world; but living with Jiddy and doing business with him day after day was a constant reminder of where the world was heading. He was repulsed by this young man who had always been his best friend; but at the same time, he could not express his true feelings to Jiddy or to anyone else, because Jiddy knew things about him that could get him killed.

People were now reporting anyone whom they suspected of being sympathetic with the aliens. For Moses, of course, the aliens and Josephat were virtually the same, and so he was innocent of feeling sympathy for them. But he had a sister and an elderly friend who were still almost certainly implicated in the movement.

The issue of Rosy's involvement had been raised in an angry crowd scene that erupted when Moses went to pick up his mail at the post office a few months earlier. He had not yet turned 22. Jiddy had been with him at the time, and had assured people that Moses had never had any contact with Rosy, from the day that she and the others had disappeared. "And Stump doesn't *want* to have any contact with her, either!" he had shouted.

That wasn't true at all, but it had been necessary for Jiddy to put it that way in order to save Moses' neck.

Others had been taken to Kakamega on as little evidence, and executed by guillotine at the soccer field there.' Moses did not regard these deaths in the same way that he did Dinah's, because these people were more than likely guilty. A few were borderline, like himself if he ever got caught, but it was all part of global peacekeeping, and he supported the belief that the occasional innocent victim was a necessary inconvenience for the overall security of the system.

Another unimaginable disaster occurred shortly after the Friday night incident with Jiddy, which temporarily distracted Moses from the depressing thoughts he had been having about the world situation. The disaster changed the thinking of many others as well.

The two aliens were reportedly angry that their followers were being executed, and so they had predicted various plagues. News reports said that all their predictions had failed, and there was no reason for anyone in Shinyalu to believe otherwise. Except for one thing: The aliens apparently continued to roam free, untouched by the authorities. Surely they must have had paranormal powers to have avoided capture for so long!

Five days before it hit, news broke that the aliens had predicted a collision between Earth and an asteroid. Scientists confirmed that there was an asteroid due to pass within millions of miles of Earth, but that the chances of it actually hitting were infinitely small.

Millions did like Moses and checked the aliens' web site 'just to be sure'. According to the aliens, their other predictions had, in fact, occurred, but there was no way for Shinyalu residents to confirm that one way or another. When the first meteorite shower actually did strike, it was just as the aliens had said it would be.

The whole top half of Africa, much of Europe, and all of the Middle East were affected by the cloud of meteors that preceded the big one. There were craters everywhere, forest fires all over Kenya and neighbouring countries, and something in the meteorites that made the water, including Lake Victoria and the Nile, highly radioactive. Hundreds of thousands of lives were lost, both through the fires and through the massive hail storms that followed the widespread burning.

But the greatest loss of life came when the asteroid itself hit somewhere in the middle of the Atlantic. It caused a shock that could be felt around the world. Huge tsunamis wiped out whole cities along the coasts of West Africa, Western Europe, and the East Coast of North and South America. All life on many islands in the Carribean was totally destroyed.

Then there was a second wave of meteorites which showered on much of Russia and Asia, with a similar loss of lives.

Several meteorites landed in maize fields and vineyards around Shinyalu, but damage was greater in the Kakamega forest, where fires spread through the vegetation, leaving a blackened scar. Giant hailstones -- some of them weighing up to a kilogram each -- resulted from the intense heat forcing them high up into the atmosphere. They killed hundreds of people in the area between Shinyalu and Kakamega alone when they finally fell. In major cities, the loss of lives was far greater.

"They've got to be stopped. Why doesn't Dangchao do something about it?" Moses complained as he and Jiddy surveyed the damage to their new house. The roof was totally destroyed, and even one wall had been knocked over from the force of the storm.

Normally Jiddy would have cautioned him about his disloyalty, but this time even Jiddy was feeling less than thrilled with how Dangchao had dealt with the aliens.

But when Dangchao did increase his efforts to stop the aliens, Moses and Jiddy were amongst those who started wishing that he had not. In the months following the asteroid, when the world should have been pouring all of its efforts into rebuilding, on a par with the unity they had shown in response to the fall of America, Dangchao was, instead, ordering all available government personnel to increase the executions, even torturing people, in an effort to get them to provide names of others who were involved in the alien movement.

The population was becoming increasingly aware that innocent people were being killed now, to appease Dangchao's rage, and to compensate for the death and destruction which had cast a pall over the whole earth. Morale which had been riding so high just a few months earlier was now at an all time low.

Both of the vehicles that Moses had been using for his *matatu* runs had been badly damaged, although they were still driveable. He could hardly charge top fares for the service he was providing now. The road, too, had been badly damaged by the storm. Most people had little money for luxuries anymore anyway, as crops had been ruined, buildings had been destroyed, and workers who had not been killed by the hail were now in danger of being executed as traitors, whether they really were traitors or not.

Good business sense, picked up from Amy seven or eight years earlier, pulled Moses through once again. He still had all the funds that he had saved up for the planned Nairobi run, and he could use them to find a way around the situation now. The answer came in undercutting his opposition. More people were returning to using *boda-bodas*, and that was forcing other *matatu* drivers out of work; but Moses had enough money to hold out even if he had to run at a loss for a year or more. He had been the first to raise fares and now he was the first to drop them, forcing other *matatu* drivers to give up and leave their customers to him.

There was suffering everywhere, and so many deaths that it was difficult for the survivors to keep up with burying them. But through it all, Moses still had enough income to take care of himself, which was the bottom line in his philosophy about life.

He lost contact with Kyme, maybe because Kyme had closed his phone account, but he still shared his thoughts with Ray, in London. Ray helped him to maintain a positive focus by urging him to count his blessings, and look on the bright side. Ray talked about God too, but it was easy for Moses to just substitue his own strong will where Ray mentioned God, and the advice still worked. The human spirit could be so amazingly resilient!

Chapter 26--Survival

Inside the cave, Amy and her family had been safe from the hailstones. But one of the first meteorites struck the side of the hill in which they lived, and caused a cave-in near the opening of the tunnel. There was still room for air to get through, but the family laboured for three days to shift enough rock to make room for them to exit the tunnel one at a time. They left most of the debris there, seeing it as yet another deterrent to intruders. The path in and out involved a bit of climbing over smaller rocks and weaving around some of the larger ones, but everyone soon learned to negotiate this course easily in the dark. Amy had the most difficulty because of her age, but she preferred the discomfort, if it made their location more secure.

The forest itself was a mess, with fallen trees everywhere, and most of the vegetation burned away, so that people moving on the road through the forest could be just made out from the hill as they walked along it. Fortunately tourism was virtually non-existent now, and the only people coming to the forest were poor villagers in search of firewood. But the family still had to stay inside the cave much of the time, and do their harvesting under cover of darkness until the trees grew new leaves.

Much of the animal life in the forest had been killed, and that included leopards. But the danger of attack at night was still very real, and they prayed constantly when gathering food. It seemed that they had miraculous protection, because in all of their time in the forest, both before and after the fires, no one was attacked.

*   *   *

Meanwhile, Moses was fighting his own battle for survival.

"I have no 1 2 talk 2," he wrote in a text to Ray. "Amy + Rosy r gone, + now I can't even talk 2 GD."

Ray knew about Jiddy's disgusting addiction to violence. Moses felt safe opening up and expressing his anger about the sacrifices to Ray without fear of being betrayed. Maybe it was the distance between them geographically, but it seemed like Ray shared his anger, even if he was more careful about expressing it.

"It's not EZ, I no," Ray wrote back. "But friendships r like that. No 1 can b there all the time. Sooner or later, every 1 will let u down."

Was Ray admitting that he didn't care either? Moses knew that if Amy had been there, she would have at least given him a hug, and a hug was what he needed at the moment. Even Kyme would have known that, but Kyme was gone too now.

"U need inner strength, Mo," Ray continued. "Something 2 carry u thru when others fail. Do you pray?"

Moses ignored the question when he replied: "I'm getn stronger. What doesn't kill me will make me stronger, rite?" And he added a winking smiley at the end of the message before typing in, "Gotta go."

In his heart, however, he felt that he had done his best to send out a plea to Ray for help, and the plea had gone unnoticed.

Chapter 27--Despair

About a year after the asteroid hit, something happened to Moses. There did not seem to be a single incident that triggered it; but the sum total of all that he was going through reached a point which finally overcame his almost superhuman ability to shut out the negatives. On his run from Shinyalu to Kakamega, he had always made a point of avoiding the soccer field where the guillotine entertained the masses in the larger city. After the horror Jiddy related about Dinah, he never returned to the theaters in the village, and he took a loss in revenue by paying another driver to do the Friday night run, so that he could avoid the markets entirely during the sacrifices. He rarely even talked to Jiddy now, and he had withdrawn into himself, even when around his customers.

Perhaps that was it. Perhaps it had been his ability to maintain positive relationships with others, most notably Jiddy, that had kept him positive about so much in the past. He certainly was finding less and less reason to be positive now, and his feelings toward himself as well as his fellow citizens was one of growing revulsion.

In relation to those around him, Moses was reasonably successful. Corruption had returned with a vengeance, and the police were back extorting money from *matatu* drivers, but Moses was still able to use his fame as the ID Mark poster boy to call the bluff of those who tried to extort from him. It is doubtful that he really had much pull with those in power, but corrupt constables were not prepared to take such a risk when they had so many other easy pickings from which to choose.

Nevertheless, the despair and horror continued to build up inside of Moses until he had to act on thoughts which had been wafting through his mind for several weeks. It was on a Tuesday afternoon, when he knew Mr. Barasa would be busy at the bank. Moses dropped his last passengers off in Kakamega, and then drove over to Barasa's house. He walked straight around to the back porch, and lifted a long crate off the single barrelled shotgun that he knew was hidden there.

Tying a knot of any sort with just one hand and a stump was a difficult feat, but Moses had prepared the string at home, when he had time to labour over it. (He did not want to lose time now, and risk being discovered.) There was a loop on one end, which he placed over the trigger and then pulled it tight. He propped the butt of the gun on the soft earth close to the edge of the porch, and sat in front of it, with the gun aimed toward his head.

He looped the string around his big toe and held the loose end in his left hand.

There was no one to write a note to. The only people who mattered, Rosy and Amy, had been taken away from him by Josephat. But he allowed himself a few brief moments to reflect on his own life before pulling the trigger. Even in the depths of despair there was a touch of positive thinking in this young man. It had not been a totally bad life, he thought. He had gone through things that others in Kenya could hardly imagine. He had lived a full life, experienced success when others were struggling just to stay alive. The tragedy was just that he had never understood where it was all leading.

The present state of the world suggested that maybe Amy was right about a curse being on all those who had followed his lead in support of the banks, the government, and the whole greedy rat race. If it was true that God was going to destroy those who had destroyed the earth, then he too deserved to be destroyed. He had continued to ignore the waste that went on during those glorious days of decadent debauchery, and when the dream had ended, he was amongst those who continued to waste far more than his share of the resources, in order to look out for himself... number one, as he used to say it. Surely, what had once been seen as only an American sin was now present in his own heart and in the hearts of others in his village.

Death by shotgun blast to the head was almost too good an end to a life that had only taken from others and rarely given anything in return. Others might not have been so harsh in their thoughts about him; Moses knew that many people liked him. Nevertheless, in his heart he knew that even his good nature was always carefully calculated to secure favours for himself... never too obvious in his manipulations of others, always maintaining that air of humility and good nature that worked so well to win friends and influence people.

He remembered a night when he had told Rosy that being nice to people was a way to get others to be nice to you. In her innocence, she had asked, "But what about God? Don't you try to be nice to people for *him*?"

How can I do something for someone I've never met?

Moses thought once again, as tears of self-pity flowed.

With that final thought in mind, he pushed his left big toe slowly away from his body. As he did, the string on the trigger moved, ever so slowly, sliding down toward the end of the curved trigger. Just as the gun erupted, he had seen it slip entirely off the trigger. A sudden movement to stop it from slipping was too late; but the gun exploded anyway, not hitting him full in the face as he had intended, but taking off the top of his head nevertheless.

Everything turned black, and stayed that way for a very long time. He was conscious of the blackness, but that was all. He was falling through it, bracing for an impact that never came. There was no way of telling how long the falling sensation lasted, or what brought it to an end, but at some stage, he found himself walking through a blackened, burned out forest, ovewhelmed with a feeling of hopelessness. All around him was a sense of death, like he was surrounded by the spirits of others who had, like him, died without hope, in the depths of despair.

Out of the smoke that hovered over the scene came an image of a face so ugly, and so evil that it sent shivers down his spine. If this was death, then death had definitely not proven to be the escape that he had longed for. He felt trapped in an eternity of hopeless depression, so intense that he could only groan pitifully. His groan was met by the groans of others out there in the darkness of the forest, others who appeared to also be trapped in this same horrible place.

His groans turned into a prayer, as he begged for release. He hated himself for never having broken down like this while still alive. He had never been desperate enough to even try talking to the God he did not know. It had been too easy to just brush such thoughts aside. And now it was too late. Surely, this was hell, and he was going to be trapped here forever, regretting the spiritual indifference that had characterised so much of the life he had once known.

But then Moses heard other voices. The voices of people talking to one another. He was in the air now, looking down on a group of people in green robes gathered around a table. The darkness receded, and he was able to see clearly the features of someone lying face-up on the table. It was himself. These were doctors, and they were fitting a metal plate to his head. There was a gaping hole where his forehead should have been. The front of his brain was missing. The metal plate was being riveted to those edges of his skull that had survived the shotgun blast.

He prayed more fervently than ever now, begging God to give him another chance, to let him live, to show him what he must do, to make his life count for something more than selfish success.

And then all was darkness once again.

Chapter 28--An Invitation

Mr. Barasa had rushed home to retrieve a forgotten briefcase, and was just pulling into the driveway when the gun went off. All of Moses' forehead was missing, and bits of his brain were splattered against the back wall of the house. The situation looked hopeless; but there was very little bleeding. Barasa gathered the young man in his arms, placed him in the back of the four-wheel-drive, and sped off to the local hospital.

Normally, the staff would not have even bothered to treat such an obviously fatal wound. But they recognised Moses as the face of the new economic system, and so, after putting him on a drip and giving him two liters of blood, they sent staff to accompany him on a one and a half hour ride to the Aga Khan Hospital, in Kisumu, on the shores of Lake Victoria. Shortly before the ambulance reached the hospital, Moses went into cardiac arrest. A doctor travelling in the back of the vehicle administered CPR until the hospital was able to get his heart started again through electro-convulsive shock.

Surgeons from Nairobi were already in the air, by the time the ambulance pulled into the Aga Khan. Surgery started late that night and continued until early the next morning. In the meantime, however, someone had leaked the story to the media, noting who it was that had received the injury. By the time plates had been fashioned and were being placed over the gaping hole, the following day, there was a small army of reporters in the hospital foyer, representing newspapers and TV stations from around the world.

The fact that Moses had been brought back to life, and that doctors were saying that he would survive the horrific "accident" was a feel-good story that the world desperately needed to hear. So much had gone wrong for Dangchao's new world order, in such a short period of time, that people needed something to rekindle hope in his failing system. Word quickly reached the Secretary General, in Jerusalem.

"It'll be some time before we know how complete his recovery will be," the head surgeon announced at a press conference, held shortly after surgery was completed. "You must remember that he has lost a large portion of his brain, and so we cannot expect too much."

Levi Xu Dangchao was watching the report on a big flat-screen TV in his throne room in Jerusalem.

"Bring him here. Bring him to me. He and I can fight this thing together," he declared. No doubt Dangchao was thinking of his own miraculous recovery after what everyone had believed was a fatal head wound. But it was not to be so dramatic for Moses.

A report came back from medical experts in Kenya:

"It will be months, before Mr. Chikati will be able to fly," the report said. "Most of the front part of his brain has been blown away. If he is able to talk at all, we expect it to be little more than a slur."

Dangchao made it clear that he wanted regular updates on Moses Chikati's progress. He still wanted the young man to be brought to Jerusalem eventually, but, in the meantime, he decided to take a trip to Kenya himself.

Dangchao arrived at the hospital a week later to be told by the medical superintendent, "Moses has surprised us all by starting to talk; but because the accident has destroyed much of the frontal lobe, his ability to feel or express emotions is virtually non-existent."

The tall, handsome world leader nodded to indicate that he had heard, but he still insisted on being allowed to visit Moses, who felt neither joy nor contempt on seeing the Secretary General enter his room. There was no need for an introduction, as the handsome leader's picture was displayed everywhere. Barely a person on earth would not have recognised him.

"I am here because I like you," Dangchao announced. "You have no family, and I have no family; so I will be your family. You can come to live with me." Dangchao smiled broadly, confident that the young man sitting up in the bed would be thrilled at his offer.

"I need no family," Moses mumbled with some difficulty. "I am twenty-four years old." He was not trying to be disrespectful. It was just that these were the facts as he perceived them.

Dangchao's eyebrows lifted as he contemplated the total lack of interest in himself... a reception that could easily have cost a person their life in any other setting.

"You think about it," Dangchao said magnanimously as he handed him a business card with his email address on it. "When you decide, I will send someone to accompany you. Everything will be provided, and everything will be first class. You will like it, I am sure."

Moses stared back blankly, through drooping eyelids.

Chapter 29--The End of Josephat

Although very few words passed through his lips, and no hint of emotion could be seen in his eyes, from the time that Moses regained consciousness there were many thoughts going through his mind. He could remember everything clearly, including the experience he had had during the hours when his life had hung in the balance, but it was like it had all happened to someone else. Moses puzzled over everything, but felt nothing. No remorse. No anger. No excitement. Nothing.

The man who essentially ruled the world had invited him to become part of his family. That much he understood. But he had no thoughts, neither positive nor negative about it. If it happened, it happened.

He remembered the horrors of human sacrifice that had led him to contemplate suicide in the first place, but took note that he no longer felt revulsion about it. His indifference to all of this now was quite possibly evidence that he had lost his soul as a result of the shotgun blast, but he felt neither panic nor remorse about that either.

One thing did intrigue him, however, and that was the deep feelings he remembered having while unconscious. They had led him to pray more earnestly than he had ever prayed before, if, indeed, he ever *had* prayed before. That experience had taken place during his encounter with death, at a time when he had already lost the front part of his brain. So how was it possible for him to have felt such deep emotion at that time? Was it only a dream... a memory of what emotions had felt

like before the accident? That was not possible, because
he had truly never experienced such intense sadness
in his entire life, not when his mother was killed, not
when he lost his arm, nor even when Rosy left.

He returned to Shinyalu, where, apart from weekly
check-ups at the Aga Khan, he was soon back driving
the *matatu*, doing budgets, and caring for himself. Everything moved more slowly for him now. He had no
desire to increase the business, and when customers
complained that his driving was too slow, it had no effect
on him. The relationship with Jiddy was much the same,
because it had already deteriorated to almost nothing
before the suicide attempt. Jiddy knew better than to
express his feelings when around Moses, and Moses
wasn't interested if he had.

"Have you heard the news?" a customer said to him
one afternoon, pushing his face up close to see if he
could catch a flicker of emotion in Moses' eyes when he
announced his bit of news. "Josephat! He's in the area.
Someone saw him over in Ileho, on the other side of the
forest."

There was the slightest flicker of interest as Moses
lifted his eyes to listen more closely. Once again, inside
his head there was memory of all the problems he had
associated with Josephat. He knew that he had hated
the man for taking Amy and Rosy away from him. He
knew that he had lived for the day when he could confront
Josephat and wring out of him the truth about Amy and
Rosy. But none of this translated into feelings... apart
from that little turn of his head. He wanted to ask what

was being done to capture Josephat, but did not even have enough interest to ask that. It did not matter, however, because the next line to come out of the customer's mouth answered the unspoken question.

"Tomorrow, the cops will start a search. They think he's been hiding in the forest. We shoulda looked there years ago. Are you goin' ta help us?" There was so little of the forest left, that the search would be a short one.

Moses just looked at him quizzically. Would he be any help, as slow as he was? For that matter, did it really make any difference whether they got Josephat or not?

"Don't know," was all he could say.

*   *   *

That night, Moses sat alone in his van, waiting for a customer. It was dark, and the village was almost deserted except for the late night theater crowd, who would be coming out at any moment. He had taken to working longer hours to make up for his slowness. Along with his indifference to what was happening in the theater, he no longer experienced fear. Other drivers disliked the risks attached to working alone after dark, but Moses was not like them. There were *boda-boda* drivers on duty, but their bikes were all locked up outside the theater while they waited safely inside.

Moses had seen no movement, and not heard a sound -- either from the theater or from anywhere else -- when the back door clicked open. He had not seen anyone approaching, and the customer spoke only one word.

"Kakamega."

A glance up at the rear-view mirror revealed the familiar felt hat that could mean only one thing. Josephat!

After more than four years of searching, Josephat had come to him. He had set himself down in the back seat and then presumed to order Moses to drive him to Kakamega at this late hour.

But Moses responded obediently, starting the engine.

The theater was just letting out, and both men knew there would be more passengers if Moses waited even one minute.

"We must go now," Josephat said flatly. Was it an order or a request? Moses did not know, but he obeyed, driving slowly away from the intersection. Some of the theater patrons could see that he was the only *matatu* driver on duty and that he was leaving. They shouted out in desperation, but he kept going... slowly. Moses could not be certain, but he thought an expression on one of the faces indicated that the man had recognised the passenger sitting directly behind him, with his face -- and that hat -- clearly visible in the window.

Maybe he would tell others. Maybe someone would come after them... if they could commandeer another vehicle.

Somewhere in the darkness, on the road to Kakamega, the *matatu* pulled over to the side of the road and stopped for a minute or two, before driving on. Later, as it came to the steep descent, leading down to the river, it slowed down. They passed two people walking down the hill in the darkness. Rain had been falling earlier in the day, and the water was flowing swiftly under the bridge now, inflated by the rains upstream. On the far side of the bridge, the vehicle stopped again. Its lights went out, after which the driver and his passenger stepped out.

"Listen!" one of the two men descending the road to the river whispered to his companion. They could barely see the vehicle in what little moonlight shone through the clouds, but there were angry shouts, an agonised scream, and then a splash in the river as the pair raced down the hill.

"What's happening down there?" the man shouted as they approached the near side of the bridge. His pace slowed to a walk, and then to a stop as he contemplated what might await him and his friend on meeting up with whoever was out there in the darkness. A bridge is a good place for robbers to trap a victim late at night.

"Everything is satisfactory now." It was Moses Chika-ti, sounding like he was giving a muffled report on the quality of his last meal and not talking about the altercation that the two men were certain they had just heard. Nevertheless, they both recognised the voice, and what he said gave them enough courage to cross over to where the *matatu* was standing.

About the same time, headlights from another *matatu* could be seen cresting the top of the hill behind them. As the vehicle approached the bridge, its lights revealed that Moses was holding a walking stick... an intricately carved stick which even the pedestrian strangers recognised as belonging to the famous eccentric, Josephat.

"Did he try to hurt you?" they asked.

"No," Moses answered. "He shouted. That was all." And then he showed that he knew more than one definition for the word that he had made famous throughout the English-speaking world. "When I *apprehended* the cane," he said, "it was easy to push him." His speech was slow and muffled, but they picked up a sense of triumph in what he was saying.

By this time the *matatu* had arrived and a load of vigilantes piled out, armed with *pangas* and torches. After hearing the story, they shone their lights down on the raging water. There was no sign of Josephat, of course. The water was too fierce.

"Over there! Look!" someone shouted, and several other flashlights moved in the same direction, where they all focused on the one image... Josephat's distinctive black felt headpiece.

When Moses was safely back in the village, and the others had finished congratulating him, he returned to his house, pulled out his laptop and typed up an email letter.

"I am ready to come now. Can you send someone to help with my carriage?"

When he checked his mail the next morning, a reply was waiting for him.

"I have arranged for an escort. Mr. Barasa will contact you in the next few hours."

Even before he had time to finish his lunch, Barasa was in the yard with his four-wheel-drive.

"You won't need to pack anything," he said. "All that you need will be provided for you when you get there."

"We will be very early for the train if we leave now," Moses stated.

"Oh, you won't be going by train this time," Barasa said with a smile and with a touch of envy in his voice. "A charter jet will meet us at the Kakamega airstrip in less than an hour.

"Your worries are over, Moses," he exclaimed. "You will never go without anything ever again." And he ruffled the young man's hair playfully. In Moses' present mental state it was easier for Barasa to think of him as the 14-year-old that he had first met so many years earlier, and not the well-travelled worldly-wise 24-year-old that he had become.

Moses showed no emotion. He just opened the door of the vehicle and slipped into the passenger seat. He did not even take the time to leave a note for Jiddy.

Chapter 30--Life in the Palace

The plane that met Moses at the airstrip in Kakamega was probably the biggest that had ever landed there. It must have been specifically designed to take off and land in a short distance, because the airstrip itself was little more than an extended football field.

Moses was the only passenger, but he had his own hostess, who not only served him food and drinks, but massaged his feet and adjusted the lighting and entertainment system to suit the young man's wishes. His wishes were few. He had no interest in watching videos, and he was content to let her choose the music, food, and drinks But the foot massage was good, and each time she asked if he had had enough, he would request more. She cheerfully and obediently complied. The massage only ended when it was time for the hostess to buckle up for landing in Tel Aviv, several hours later.

When they arrived at their destinaton, they were greeted by a man only a few years older than Moses who was dressed like a bank manager. "Welcome to Tel Aviv!" he said. "My name is Moshe, and I will be your companion. If you have need of anything, you should just ask me, and I will tend to it."

The new arrival was taken by limousine to the palace in Jerusalem, and shown to his quarters. Moshe stood with his feet apart and his hands clasped behind his back as Moses inspected the spacious bedroom. It came with a small library along one wall, massive desk, leather lounge, fridge, bar, and state of the art entertainment system. And that was just the bedroom. It was quite late in the day, and so Moshe promised to show Moses around the rest of the palace the next morning.

"If you have need of anything during the night, just pull this cord," he said, reaching out toward a thick golden rope that hung from somewhere up in the ceiling. I will be in the room next door, and I will come to you immediately."

So much had happened and so much had changed since Moses had first experienced Western luxuries in Chicago, at the age of 14. At that time, every little novelty had come charged with excitement, wonder, and, in some cases, a little fear. Now he was ten years older, and totally impervious to all that he saw, even though the luxuries were more impressive than ever. He believed that he should be there. That was all. But he had no idea why.

The next day, Moses was taken around the rest of the palace, which was equipped with every possible comfort. Nothing in the whole building showed even the slightest signs of wear. In the afternoon, there was a brief tour of the area between the palace and the Temple Mount. He and Moshe rode in the same limousine that had met him at the airport.

"This will be your own private limousine," Moshe had told him. "If you have need of anything, a driver will be on duty to take you there at any time of the day or night." This news, too, left him unimpressed.

"You will be able to get anything that you want, even

without the mark," Moshe continued. The horrific wound had blown away Moses' microchip implant.

Back in Shinyalu, after the accident, Moses had been able to collect payment from customers, using his scanner. But when it came to him *spending* money, there had been some uncertainty within the village, and especially in Kakamega about what he should do. However, in the months between his time in hospital and his departure for Jerusalem, those who recognised him had simpy extended him credit, buoyed by the announcement that the General Secretary had visited the hospital, and by the rumour that he had invited Moses to come and live with him. As they had all been hoping, Barasa later made sure that anyone who had helped Moses was amply rewarded.

But Moshe told Moses that in Jerusalem, and shortly, anywhere else in the world, he would be able to purchase anything at all, just by using Danchao's name. He had no need of a mark, either in his missing hand or in his now missing forehead. Locals had already been informed, and soon (when Dangchao found time for a press conference to deal with the matter), anyone in the world would be expected to recognise him as being part of Levi Xu Dangchao's royal family. Moses tested it out by getting a few clothes, but other than that, he had little interest in buying anything, since he had more than he needed back at the palace anyway.

Moses never saw Dangchao himself until almost two weeks after he arrived, and then it was almost by chance, as they passed in the hallway.

"Ah, Moses Chikati! So good to see you," the Secretary-General exclaimed when he saw him.

"Hello," Moses said quietly.

"So how is everything? Are they taking good care of you? Do you like it here?"

"I have all that I need," Moses answered haltingly. He added a drawn out, "Thank you."

"We have a press conference planned for next Thursday," Dangchao announced. "I want the world to know that you are my son. Moshe will tell you what to say."

In fact, Moshe had been preparing him for more than a week already. There was a speech therapist, working overtime to improve on his voice, but Moses' primary duty at the palace had been to work with a physiotherapist who had been assigned the task of getting his facial muscles to form a smile. He could now make the corners of his lips draw up into his cheeks, enough to create a reasonable imitation of his trademark grin. The main problem, however, was that he still had to consciously will himself to do it; there was nothing spontaneous about it, because he had no sensations to make him *feel* like smiling.

But Moshe had conditioned Moses to hear and respond to a signal that was only just barely audible to the human ear. Using this signal, Moshe could get him to make the smile at appropriate spots in the speech, which he (Moshe) had prepared. Together they might be able to convince the world that the old Moses was still alive.

Chapter 31--The Entertainment Hall

Moses spent most of his time in his room, where (when not sleeping or sitting motionless in a soft chair) he would browse through the books that had been placed there. Novels were of no interest now, whether based on truth or fiction. He could not relate to any of the characters, and even if he could, he had no interest in what they were going through, just as he had no interest in what *he* was going through. But he did have a casual interest in some of the reference books, especially those with plenty of pictures.

He left his room for most meals, and often on the way to or from the cafeteria, on the far side of the palace, where he usually ate by himself, he would check out some of the other rooms. The palace staff had been briefed to ignore his occasional interruptions to business meetings (which never held Moses' attention for more than a few seconds anyway). But, between therapy sessions, he spent time in and around the heated pool, where he learned that he could get more free massages.

On the morning of Moses' second day there, Moshe had pointed out the huge hall where Dangchao offered free entertainment to visiting diplomats each evening. Moses had not been back there until one Sunday evening, two weeks after he first arrived in Jerusalem... the day after he bumped into Dangchao in the hallway. The evening meal had finished a bit later than usual that night, and he was returning to his room, when he heard a noise, like someone was in pain, coming through one of the many almost soundproof doors that led to the hall.

The young man pushed through the door and entered a small stadium; but the sound had stopped by the time he entered. A hundred or more people, mostly men, sat around the perimeter of a smoke-filled room, overlooking a big oval-shaped stage that was a good ten feet below them. Empty seats at the back of the room were much higher than those at the front. Moses moved down to the gold railing on which arms and chins were resting, so he could get a closer look at what was happening down in the polished timber pit that served as a stage.

Below them, on the stage, someone was putting body parts into a wheelie bin, including the head and torso of what must have been a young boy, still in his teens. Moses guessed that it must have been the dying screams of this same boy that had caught his attention. He sat down in a seat near the railing and continued to watch as the cart was taken away, and as the stage was sprayed clean of blood by water coming from little jets built into the sides of the entertainment area. Everything disappeared down a drain in the middle.

"And now for some lighter entertainment of a sexual nature," said a voice over the speaker system.

There was almost a groan of dissatisfaction from many of those in the audience. Most viewers moved away from the rail, to rest their backs.

Moses must have looked confused, because a middle-aged woman in the seat next to him turned and spoke to him as if she knew she was explaining things to a novice.

"It's always like this on Sundays," she said apologetically. "Something to do with organising the sacrifices. Someone's day off, I think. Instead of sacrifices, they mostly do the same old sex shows. It'll be more than half an hour before they do another sacrifice."

"What do *you* come for?" Moses asked politely.

"Oh, I come for *him*," the woman effused, and she nodded her head toward an ornate throne on the opposite side of the arena. It was empty, but Moses guessed that it was for Dangchao.

"Most people watch the shows on TV these days," the woman said, "Or they go to the Temple during the week. Only diplomats get to see him here. It's not the same if you watch him on TV. You have to be here in person to get the full effect."

Diplomats had reasonable access to Dangchao in his role as Secretary-General, so Moses wondered why this woman would be making such a big deal over seeing him in person. But she was not the only one who wanted to be there to see Dangchao. Over the next few minutes others started to enter the hall, filling up the vacant seats. Curiosity was not a part of his new personality, but Moses had nothing else to do and he was not tired. So he chose to stay a bit longer.

"The Secretary-General comes on at eight o'clock each Sunday; it's the only night he appears here. Every other night he goes to the Temple shows," the woman continued, with her hands clasped over her heart like a starry-eyed teenager. Her eyes rolled upward as she tried to imagine (or perhaps to remember) how it would be when the man of her dreams made his appearance. "It's too hard to get close to him at the Temple, but here we are only a few metres away."

The half-hour of live sex that preceded Dangchao's appearance was far more than live sex. It involved animals, rape, children, and some audience participation. But, as Moses had observed ever since his strange recovery at the Aga Khan, none of this fazed him. He knew it was wrong. He knew it would have sickened him in the past. But he was a different person now... with only an academic interest in what was happening all around him. He took more interest in the arrival of new spectators, turning to gawk each time another door opened, as he took in the actions of the "entertainers" down below.

There was, for his part, little to interest him when Dangchao came out also, despite great fanfare from an invisible orchestra. By this time, at least three or four hundred diplomats had squeezed into the tiny arena, and they were totally silent in anticipation. While Moses had enough memory to understand that spectators would find the atrocities exciting, he still could not understand what was the special attraction about Dangchao himself.

Suddenly there was a deafening roar, and every spectator in the stadium dropped to their knees in the space between their seats and the ones in front of them... everyone, that is, except for Moses Chikati. The raspy roar was coming from Dangchao's face, which had changed to the face of a creature that was half-animal and half human. His expression was so horrible that the reaction

from everyone else in the room was totally understandable to Moses as he looked on from his unique perspective. Dangchao had not noticed that Moses was in the
hall until this happened, and then it was not clear whether he was angry with the young man for his indifference,
or whether he was proud of him as his "son".

Moses was not thinking about Dangchao's reaction at
all, however, for his mind was occupied with a search for
where he had seen that same hideous face before. And
then it came to him. It was the face that had appeared
in the clouds of smoke over the burnt out forest in his
near-death experience. Dangchao (or whatever it was
that was manifesting itself through Dangchao's body at
that particular moment) had been present in his near-
death dream... if it really was a dream.

Moses simply rose to his feet and walked out through
the same door he had used to enter the arena. He wandered casually back to his room while pondering this
simple observation. If there was anything more that
Dangchao said or did during his TV appearances, Moses
did not know, nor did he have any interest in knowing.
He never returned to the entertainment hall.

Chapter 32--The Alien

"Here! In the Palace! One of the aliens!"

Moses was just finishing breakfast in the cafeteria the next morning, when a young office worker sat down at the table next to him, with news for others at that table that one of the aliens had just been captured at the airport, trying to hijack a plane. "They're bringing him here now," the informant explained. Moses got up from his chair and walked over to the table where the announcement had been made. Because the people seated there were all staff members, and because they all recognised him, they did nothing to stop Moses from listening in.

"They're bringing him here?" asked a woman at the table nervously. "But he could kill us!"

The man next to her gave a little poke with his elbow as he glanced quickly toward Moses. Locals had come to think of Moses as Dangchao's son, even though the young man had hardly even met his benefactor. In the minds of most palace workers, anything said to Moses would be passed on to Dangchao.

"Obviously, Dangchao is going to use him as bait... to get the other one here," the elbow-jabber piped in. "Don't worry, Naomi, Dangchao knows what he's doing. He's the most awesome leader the world has ever known. Take it from me, we're safe as virgins in chastity belts." The others laughed nervously. They were clearly not convinced.

In the palace? Moses thought to himself, as he tried to imagine where Dangchao would put the alien.

He turned and walked away from the table, then wandered the corridors of the palace in search of the alien, before coming to a room that had special U.N. troops guarding it. The soldiers recognised Moses, and so, when he indicated that he wanted to go in, they did what they would not have done for anyone else in the world at that moment... they let him in without a pass.

"Where's your partner?" Dangchao growled.

Moses could see only the back of a chubby man with long brown hair, who was seated facing Dangchao.

"I don't know," the man answered quietly.

He doesn't look like an alien to me, thought Moses. *He's just a harmless old man.*

"Maybe I should hold you here for a few days and see if he turns up."

The alien said nothing.

"We could have some fun with you."

"And God could have some fun with you!" the alien shot back. There was an air of authority in the man's voice. Perhaps he was not entirely harmless after all. But there was something else in his voice which was even more significat. He had an accent... an Australian accent.

It sounds so much like Kyme, Moses thought to himself; but then any male Australian accent would have sounded like Kyme's, since Kyme was the only Australian he knew apart from Winky.

But from what Moses could see over the back of the seat, the man did look a lot like Kyme... a bit greyer, perhaps, and a bit heavier than Moses had remembered Kyme to be, but very much like him, all the same.

Dangchao spoke. "I was only kidding," he said.

He's afraid of him, Moses thought. But Dangchao went on.

"I just want to ask your friend some questions. We really need to work *together*... for the good of the whole world."

Moses changed his thinking once again. Dangchao was not afraid at all. The staffer in the cafeteria was correct. He was diplomatically using one alien as bait to attract the other. But surely the aliens would know that, and they would not fall for such a trick.

Just then, the alien turned in Moses' direction, as though he had been aware all along that Moses was watching him. He looked deeply into Moses' expression-less eyes for a second or two, smiled, and then winked, before turning in the opposite direction and walking to-ward the door on the far side of the room. He did not even wait for clearance from the Secretary-General.

"Go with him!" Dangchao said to an aide, and the man raced to catch up with the palace guest.

"I'll show you to your room," the aide said as he ap-proached the alien.

For Moses Chikati, however, the man would never be thought of as an alien again. He was, instead, Kyme Rosenberg, Moses' personal friend and advisor, with whom he had lost contact a couple of years earlier!

The young man's mental faculties were such that he could not experience shock, fear, disappointment, or anything more than a slight increase in curiosity in response to what he had just observed, but it did not stop his mind from sifting through events in his past as he sought an explanation for how a kindly old Quaker from Australia could be the alien monster that had threatened to undermine all that the United Nations Secretary-General had done to prosper and stabilise the nations of the world.

Moses left by the same door through which he had entered. It was around the corner from the one that Kyme had used, and so by the time he reached the hallway on that end of the room, Kyme and Dangchao's assistant had apparently disappeared around yet another corner somewhere down the long corridor. Moses wanted to see Kyme, but only just. He was struggling with an urge to just forget about it. What difference did it make how Kyme had come to be there? There were books to read in his room, and exercises that Moshe had laid out for him to do. But in the end, he decided that the exercises were not important, and he just wandered down one hallway after another looking for his old friend instead.

Half an hour later, and Moses had backtracked all the way to where Kyme had first disappeared. He discovered that the guards who had been outside the interrogration room were now outside the room immediately next to it. Moses reached out with his good arm to open the door, but he was stopped by one of the guards.

"Sorry, we can't let you go in this time, son. It's too dangerous."

Moses was about to say, "But he's my friend," when he suddenly lost interest and wandered off toward his own room.

Chapter 33--Another One

For the next three days, Moses had no further interest in seeing Kyme, or in finding answers to the questions that lay dormant in his brain. He knew there was a serious mix-up and he wanted to talk to Kyme if he could, but he had none of the overpowering urgency about it that you or I might feel. He was content to forget about it, unless circumstances changed in such a way as to let him meet up with his old friend from Australia.

On Thursday, circumstances did exactly that.

Thursday was the day when he was to have given his speech to the media, complete with plastic smiles choreographed by Moshe. But at the last minute it was called off. Moses asked Moshe why it had been cancelled, not because it made any difference to him, but just to show polite interest.

"It's a problem with the aliens," Moshe replied. "The other one is on his way here."

Just then, there was a rumble that shook the whole palace. Both men stretched their arms out to maintain balance. The damage to his brain had slightly affected his balance, and so Moses crashed to the ground, where he lay for a few seconds before climbing slowly back to his feet, with help from Moshe.

As the rumble eased, the latest bit of news from Moshe started to sink in. *Dangchao's plan has worked,* Moses thought to himself. *The other alien is going for the bait.* And then he remembered Kyme. *Wait a minute. Kyme isn't an alien; so who could this second person be?*

He had previously thought that Josephat was one of the aliens; but after that night on the bridge, he knew it could not be the man who had taken his sister and Winky away from him. But could there be a link between Kyme and the *real* aliens?

Moses dismissed himself from Moshe, relieved that he would not have to perform for the Press, and he continued to aimlessly wander the halls, as he had been doing when Moshe tracked him down. He thought back over all that he knew about the aliens and all that he knew about Kyme, but still could find no link.

A few minutes later, while approaching the room where Kyme was being held, he saw the door open, and two soldiers in U.N. uniforms come out, followed by Kyme, and then two more U.N. soldiers. They turned to walk on ahead of him, but his eyes and Kyme's eyes crossed in that split second before Kyme turned. Moses thought he picked up another wink. Was Kyme playing a game with him?

He continued walking behind his friend and the four soldiers, but fell further behind as they moved with a certainty that he lacked. Nevertheless, he did see the cluster of soldiers push out through the front doors of the palace, and he pulled out the special beeper he used to call his limo, something he had only done on two or three occasions since coming to the Palace, and then only for the experience of getting outside for a while.

"I am at the front entrance," he mumbled to the driver. Can you pick me up there?"

The limo was just pulling up when Moses pushed open the front door of the palace. He moved as quickly as he was able, which was not very quickly, down the wide stone steps. *Perfect timing* he thought.

A crowd of people moving slowly away from the Palace was his best clue as to where Kyme and the alien might be.

"Follow those people," Moses said to the driver, pointing in the direction of the crowd.

The driver said nothing, but drove slowly along the road leading up to the palace, until he was almost touching people at the edge of the crowd. They continued inching along like that for a few blocks, until someone from the crowd finally got the message and called on people to move aside and give the vehicle access to the two men who were the center of everyone's attention.

They were near a fountain, and so the two men sat on a bench facing the narrow roadway. The limo pulled up directly in front of them, and Moses rolled the window down. He leaned his chin on the stump of his right arm, which cushioned the edge of the open window.

Both men smiled toward him, and that is when the mystery deepened for Moses. Sitting next to Kyme was Ray, his good friend and other father figure from London. Still, in Moses' voice there was little surprise, and there was not much more in the voices of his friends either.

"Hello," Moses said, and they echoed his greeting with a wave of their hands. "What are you doing here?" he asked.

"We're working for God," Rayford said. "We've been praying for you."

"Did you know I was here?"

"Yes, we heard from our people here in Israel before we left," Rayford continued. "It seems like half of Jerusalem knows about you being here."

The look on Moses' face was one of puzzlement throughout much of the conversation; mention of "their people" made him squint his eyes even more, in an effort to understand what Rayford meant.

"Did you come to see me?" he asked.

"No," they both replied simultaneously. "We had other more important business," Kyme finished off.

"Are you the aliens?"

"Do we look like aliens?" Kyme asked with a big smile.

Moses paused before he said, "I don't know what aliens look like. You're my friends."

"We *are* teaching people about a different world," Kyme explained. "A world where God is the king, and where people love each other."

"Can I go there?" Moses asked, without showing any serious interest.

"You can if you will just follow your heart," Ray responded.

"I don't have a heart now," Moses said, with something close to sadness in his voice. "I have no feelings. I died, you know. I went to hell. Dangchao was there."

It took ever so long for Moses to say all of this, speaking very slowly as he did, with a slight spastic slur; but neither of the men interrupted, and the crowd was totally silent as he spoke.

"Do you want to see this new world?" Rayford asked, compassion showing in his voice.

"I don't want anything. That is the way I am now," Moses replied.

"Oh but you *do* want things," Kyme said. "Why are you here now? Why are you talking to us? Isn't it because you wanted to talk to us."

"But I know you," Moses said.

"And you can know God too," Kyme answered. "Have you tried talking to him?"

"I did when I was dead," Moses answered more quickly than had been his earlier responses. Then he reverted to his slow drawl. "But it's too late now."

"It may be; but have you *tried*?" Kyme continued.

Moses remembered something from his death dream. He had felt something very strongly then. In the dream he had remembered with the deepest regret that he never even *tried* to talk to God when he had been alive. And it dawned on him that he had not tried to talk to God since either. He knew of one time when he had tried to do something good after coming back to life, but that was not the same as talking to God.

"What do I say?" he asked.

"Anything you want to say," Kyme replied. "And take

time to listen too. God doesn't always use words, but he has ways to let you know he's there."

"Just don't try to tell him what to do." Ray interjected.

"That's true," Kyme went on. "Some people want God to do what they say, before they'll become his friends. But even when he *does* do what they ask for, they don't usually change their ways for him."

Just then a message came over the chauffeur's two-way radio.

"Sorry, sir, but we have to return," the driver said to Moses over his shoulder.

"We are going now," Moses announced to his friends, with no sign of disappointment.

Ray and Kyme stood to their feet and looked on sadly as the limo pulled away.

"Please try it!" Kyme shouted as Ray waved. Moses just rested his chin on the window ledge and looked blankly back at them.

Then he sat back in the seat and in the short drive to the Palace he decided to do what they had suggested. Words formed in his mind:

Hi God. This is me. I want to be your friend. I don't know how to do it. Can you show me?

He sat and waited. He saw nothing and felt nothing.

That's OK, he said after a brief pause. *I still want to be your friend.*

Chapter 34--The Press Conference

Back at the Palace, Moshe was waiting at the curb when the limo pulled up.

"We must move quickly," he said. "The press conference is back on... We're due there at three o'clock."

It was pointless telling Moses that anything needed to be done quickly. He had one speed, and it was slow. But he made no protest at Moshe's prodding, and took the script that was handed to him as he was marched off toward the conference room.

"In here first. Comb your hair and tuck in your shirt!" Moshe was pointing him toward the men's room, as he handed him a comb. Moses took the opportunity to use the toilet as well, and he was characteristically slow in finishing his ablutions.

Then Moshe sat him down on a couch in the hall, just outside the room where members of the Press were already interviewing Dangchao on another matter.

"You don't have to read it out loud here and now, but can you go over it in your head one more time before we go in?" Moshe asked. "Just so it will be fresh in your mind and you won't stumble on the words."

Moses agreed, and proceeded to read the script, although he kept getting distracted and had to be directed back to the paper. There were little smilies written into the script, as reminders for Moses to "smile". If he should forget, or if his eyes should stray from the page (since he had ██████████████████ by now), Moshe had a gadget that would send out a high-pitched signal, almost imperceptible to the human ear, which would cause Moses to smile almost involuntarily. The young man had endured three sessions a day for the past two weeks in order to develop this skill.

I want to be your friend. Please show me how. Inside his own head, Moses was still working on what Kyme and Ray had told him to do earlier, and it was interfering with his concentration. Moshe could see that Moses was distracted, but today was D-day, whether they were ready or not, and so they would just have to hope for the best.

They entered the room quietly, without disrupting what was already underway. Media representatives were quizzing Dangchao on something that had happened just before he let Kyme and Ray go free to walk the streets of Jerusalem.

"How many soldiers were killed?" a reporter asked.

"No one was killed, although there were a few injuries from the earthquake."

"But the flames. What about the flames?" asked the same reporter.

"Next?" Dangchao said calmly as he looked for questions from other members of the Press corps. It was like he never heard the other man's second question. An aide approached the reporter and quietly asked him to leave the room.

"I'm sorry. I meant nothing by it," he protested in a whisper.

"Come outside and we can discuss it. We will only be a minute."

There was a look of terror in the reporter's eyes, while fellow journalists and camera people averted their attention away from him, acting as though they were unaware of what was happening.

"What are your plans for the aliens?" another reporter asked cautiously.

"We will give them some time to consider their options before we act. They are completely under my control at the moment," Dangchao said confidently. "Their reign of terror is over... finished, and they know it.

"But we have some other good news," the Secretary-General announced, looking up at Moshe and Moses, who were standing by the door at the back of the room. "For three weeks now, the young man who has been the face of the new economy has been living here in the Palace with me, as my own son. As you all know, like me, Moses Chikati miraculously returned from certain death, and he is here today to talk to you."

Dangchao still wore a black patch over his left eye as a reminder of the assassin's attack three and a half years earlier. The world mourned for him for almost 24 hours, before he miraculously revived.

"It is ironic that Moses Chikati, who encouraged so many millions of people to face their 'apprehensions' and get the microchip implant over the past seven years, is now the only person on earth unable to have a mark, either in his right hand or in his forehead. But, because of his great service to the new world order, I have made him a member of my family, and, like myself, he need only show his face and utter my name, and business people all over the world should provide him with whatever he needs. This is my decree, and I expect everyone to honour it."

Dangchao motioned for Moses to come join him on the small stage where he was sitting. He continued to speak as the young man weaved his way through the reporters.

"When I first visited Moses in Kenya, the hospital authorities said it would be many months before he would be able to talk, and then it would be almost unintelligible. But I want the world to see what my powers and the best technology that money can buy have done to bring life back into someone who lost more than twenty percent of his brain in a horrible hunting accident earlier this year."

Dangchao and others had been successful in hiding from the world the real reason for the "accident" and how the wound had been inflicted; and the media knew better than to ask questions which might uncover it.

Moses stepped up onto the small stage.

"Moses has a speech which he has prepared for you today. Come here, Moses." And Dangchao stood to greet Moses and to give him more room on the couch. Moses took a seat, shielding his eyes as he adjusted to the bright lights, then placed the paper in his lap, and waited for a signal to begin.

"Go ahead, son," Dangchao said in his kindest voice.

Moses cleared his throat.

"It is a miracle that I am sitting here today," he read, followed by a wide smile, which he held for just a second or two, as the cameras flashed. Moshe and Dangchao shared the momentary success through a secret glance at one another. It was working already. The media loved Moses. He was speaking even more clearly than he had in his latest practice runs.

"I was as good as dead when I arrived at the hospital in Kenya."

And then Moses stopped. This was where he was supposed to tell the world that Dangchao's spiritual presence in the hospital, even before he arrived there in person, was what pulled him through. It was not time yet for a smile, but Moses seemed to be stuck. Moshe waited for a few seconds and then clicked his signal. Moses smiled, but it did not have the same effect as the first one. It did, however, kick Moses into action, for after he held the smile for a few seconds, he started speaking again, although he was not reading from the script how.

"I am only here today because of the *interventions* I received from my friend," he said.

Not the exact words, but close enough, thought Moshe and Dangchao simultaneously. They could see that if Moses used his own words, the speech would look even more convincing.

"I want to tell you about my friend," Moses said. And here he managed to insert a smile without help from Moshe or from his notes. He was performing perfectly.

"I think that my friend has the answers to all of our *predicaments*... my predicaments... your predicaments... and the predicaments of the whole world."

His voice was still emotionless, and his speech was slow, but in some ways it added to the impact of what he was saying. People watching would be trying to experience for themselves the feeling behind his words, even as Dangchao and Moshe were doing in the press room.

"My friend is... is all-powerful... He is with me here now. He is helping me to say what I am saying. I do not deserve a friend like this."

Moshe thought this was a good place to insert a smile and so he clicked his gadget and Moses responded, holding the smile until he was ready to start again.

"You can find help from this friend too... where you are. But first you have to ask. Just ask. That is all I did. I asked."

Moshe and Dangchao both registered confusion on their faces, about what Moses was getting at, and about where he was taking the worldwide live audience. The arrival of the two aliens in Jerusalem had been the biggest news since the asteroid, and so every network in the world was linked in to this broadcast. This was far more than the usual weekly press conference for Dangchao.

"The *aliens* are my friends too. They told me that *God* can be my friend. I asked him..."

Dangchao jumped off the couch and out of camera range. "Stop it! Stop it now!" he whispered loudly, as his face started to change. "Turn off the cameras."

"I asked him, and he *inspirited* me to say this," Moses continued.

What was happening to the camera people? They seemed unable (or unwilling) to move. Was it their instinct for news... in particular, the shocking news that Dangchao's adopted "son" was now supporting his enemies? Or was there some supernatural power holding them back from obeying the order?

"Kill him! Kill him!" Dangchao shouted, so loudly now that it would have been picked up by every microphone in the room. The cameras continued to roll. Some even turned to catch the world ruler's demonic rage, and then swung back to Moses, just as Dangchao shouted again, "Shoot! Gaddamit! Shoot him!"

Three shots rang out just as a smile spread across Moses' face. It was not his usual mischievous grin. Instead, it was the contented smile of an angel.

And then, just as the last vestiges of life flowed from his face, a tear magically appeared at the corner of one eye, and trickled slowly down his face. He then slumped forward and fell in a heap on the floor.

The master TV camera finally stopped with just the image of Moses, the smile, and the tear somehow frozen on the screen, as though someone had hit "pause" when they should have hit "stop".

Chapter 35--Kakamega Forest

The world had become worse than numb to the sufferings of others; many, like Jiddy, had come to actually find pleasure in it. However, there was something different about Moses' death, watched by hundreds of millions, if not billions, both on the live broadcast and on replays over the next few hours, before Dangchao succeeded in getting it taken off all but the most remote stations.

There were a few hundred people (a tiny percentage in the bigger picture) who made an eleventh hour decision to stand against the Dangchao regime, even if it meant being beheaded. They each did what Moses had done. They dared to talk to his Friend, asking if they too could become Friends with the one who had brought peace to Moses Chikati. It was the young man's calm acceptance of his fate, the beatific smile, and that one tear. The world needed what he had.

But for these other converts, the newly discovered Friendship was far more emotional than it had appeared to be for Moses. They had been hardening their conscience for years, closing their ears to the truth. Those tears of remorse that Moses had shed in his near death experience were multiplied many times over in the prayers of sincere repentance that issued from those final citizens of the heavenly City.

The killings went on, right up to the end. Kyme and Ray were also killed, just six days after Ray had arrived in the unholy city of Jerusalem. Many of the secret hideouts of their followers around the world were discovered as well, with tragic consequences.

But there was one hideout back in Kenya that remained secure right up to the end, thanks to something Moses had done earlier.

*   *   *

"Tell us the story again, Josh!"

It was raining outside the cave, and all the children (most of them grown now) were huddled together inside the main room, with a few candles illuminating them. Three days earlier, they had buried Amy, who died peacefully in her sleep, from an unknown illness.

They all knew about the Two Witnesses (as Ray and Kyme were known amongst the underground movement that had been led by them over the past seven years). They didn't know their names, what they looked like, or that Moses had anything to do with either of them, but they did know that the Two Witnesses had both gone to Jerusalem over the past few days. They also knew that they were nearing the end of the suffering and persecution that believers in God had been facing for the past three and a half years.

About the time that Ray had left London and Kyme had left Sydney, each on their separate way to Jerusalem, Josh and the older children had returned to the forest, knowing that they would not leave again until their salvation arrived.

Destruction of the forest had continued, right up to the end, and it had become harder and harder for them to grow enough to feed themselves. They were totally out of food now, and had been so since burying Amy.

This tiny young army believed that a cosmic event marking the end of an era of evil and corruption, was going to turn the tables, and make them rulers over a new world of peace and love. It was a laughable fairytale in a world that had lost all faith in God and almost all ability to tell right from wrong. Nevertheless, the young people (and one not-so-young man) had been waiting in the cave for several days now, counting the hours.

"Please, Josh!" Karla repeated. "Tell us the story about how you saw Moses." Karla was 13 now.

The boxes of literature were long gone, but the children seated themselves on old rabbit skin rugs in anticipation. Rosy always enjoyed hearing this story the most.

"I knew they was looking for me," Josephat began. "And I figgered they knew I was in the forest. I had to do something real quick, to stop them coming here."

"How did you know they were looking?" asked Jane, one of the twins. No matter how many times he told the story, there were always new questions... things that had been left out in previous tellings.

"Good question," Josephat replied. "I didn't know for absolute *sure*, but I was walking through Ileho in the middle of the night, headin' toward the forest. It's so dark there I never had problems with being seen before. But I tripped over someone sleeping off a drunk on the side of the road. He woke up scared real bad; then jumped up to fight me. I was already on the ground from the fall, so I just barely got away. But he sayed or did something in the scuffle that made me think he knew me... maybe from the cane or from something that I sayod."

"Tell about Moses," Karla said.

"He will. Just be patient," 13-year-old Jo-Jo chided.

"So the next night, I sneaked into Shinyalu to see what I could learn. I was thinking about turning myself in, if they knew and if they was coming this way... you know, to stop them coming here. That's when I saw Moses sitting in his *matatu* all alone, outside the pictures.

"I got in and told him to take me to Kakamega. I just wanted to get out of town, away from the people, and see what I could learn from him.

"Sure enough, they was talking about a search of the forest, to start the next day.

"But Moses sounded different... like he wanted to help us. He asked how Amy and Rosy was, and if I had hurt them. I sayed you was all safe, and God was helping us. Then he asked if he could help us in some way.

"That's when the idea popped into my head."

"You mean it really just came like that, all at once?" Lucy asked. Lucy was 17 now.

"Kinda. I was thinkin' 'bout a lot of plans. Like when Moses pulled away from the village, some people came out of the theater and so I let them see me. I wanted them to think I was in Kakamega... anywhere but in the forest. But I was open to them catching up and killing me too, if it would stop the hunt.

"But then I took a chance and told Moses that I needed to make people think I was dead, so's they would stop looking. I sayed it would help protect the rest of you, and he didn't question me on it one bit. Jist joined right in.

There was a big rock at the side of the road, so we pulled over and picked it up after I told him my idea. He was a little slow takin' it in, but by the time we reached the river, he had it clear enough to pull it off."

"Did you pass anyone else on the road?" asked Lucy.

"Not that I can remember. It was too late for anyone to be out walking. God musta put those two men there by the bridge just at the perfect time. We had to drive to the far side to give us enough time to get the rock out, do some shoutin', and then push it over the edge into the water. I cut myself and put some blood on the head of the cane before we stopped. So Moses took the cane, and then I dropped my felt hat where it would land on the side of the river, before I raced off into the dark. I stayed hiding all that day, and come back here the next night."

"Well, it sure worked," said Micah, who, at 22, was the oldest of the children. "We haven't had any problems with them hunting around here since."

"Josh, do you think Moses will make it?" Rosy asked.

"You've asked me that so many times," Josephat complained. "You know I can't say. He did take the mark, you know."

"But the papers say he blowed it off his head in an accident," the other twin reminded him.

"The papers say a lot of things, Gene," Josephat responded. "They also sayed that he went to live with Dangchao. Like I sayed before, only God knows."

Just then a strange hum flowed down the tunnel from the cave entrance. It was like the most beautiful organ music anyone could imagine. They all stood to their feet and turned in the direction from which it was coming.

"Wow! What's that?" exclaimed Karla, who was the first to push through the heavy curtain to the tunnel. Normally they would have all gone instinctively silent if there had been any disturbance outside.

Josephat said nothing, but he and the others followed. Out in the tunnel, where they could all find their way in total darkness, there was a faint glow that seemed to accompany the musical hum. This, too, was the sort of thing that would have sent them deeper into hiding under any other circumstances. But this was different. Very different.

There were rocks and other debris from when the meteor had hit the mountain and caused a cave-in, but they were almost dancing over all of this now, on their way out of the cave. Each of them, Josephat included, was so happy that they were almost laughing. They felt changes... good changes... taking place inside their bodies, and their clothing was changing too, turning a brilliant white.

Out in the night air, where the rain had now stopped, they all gathered in a circle at the cave entrance, and joined hands. Karla was the first to actually start laughing, and soon they were all intoxicated with joy. Whatever was happening, it was making them feel... well, the only word for it was "high", and it became even more appropriate as they suddenly found themselves rising up off the ground.

"Are we going crazy?" Micah asked. "I feel like I can fly."

"I think it's the rapture," said Josephat.

"The rapture?" Jane exclaimed. The word had fallen into disrepute with them, because so many church people had used it to describe an imaginary escape from all that this band of saints had experienced over the past three and a half years.

"It really means being so happy that you feel like you are floating on air," Josephat shouted across the circle, which had grown much bigger now that they had released each other's hands. "But it's mostly used for a Bible teaching about floating up into the sky to meet Jesus."

"Wow! Jesus? Where?" Lucy shouted as she looked in all directions at once. Surely the noise they were making could be heard across the forest in the stillness of the night, but worries about being discovered by neighbours were now suddenly not a part of their thinking.

Fifteen-year-old Simon was the first to give in to an urge to experiment with his new flying ability.

"Hey, look at Simon!" Karla shouted, pointing across the circle at him. The others looked as Simon bent his body in such a way as to make it veer off from the circle and enter an orbit of its own. He bent again and then zoomed up above them. Soon others were doing similar stunts, as their laughter rang through the darkness. Their bodies had all taken on that glow they had detected in the cave, and so it looked like a scene from

Peter Pan as all the children darted around the sky like a lantern full of fireflies. Even Josephat, who suddenly looked much younger, was joining in.

A moment later they became aware of other creatures off in the distance doing something similar. While they were all turned in that direction, another presence moved silently up from behind them.

"Youse had better get a move on; we've got a lot of travelling to do." It was Winky! Much younger, and full of life. The twitch in her eye was gone too.

All those who had appeared to be surfing gentle breezes manouvered their bodies in such a way as to converge back where Amy was hovering.

"This way!" Amy said, and she turned north. About the same time, it became clear that dim lights off in the distance were also moving in the same direction, converging slightly as they progressed. The air was neither hot nor cold and breathing was not a problem, even though they must have been travelling at more than a hundred miles an hour by this time.

The journey went on through the night, without the slightest hint of anyone feeling tired. It was all so exciting and unbelievable. As they moved closer to the other lights, they found some that they recognised... people from the various underground bases that Josephat and the older children had visited and supported on a regular basis. Farther along, they met up with more whom they had never met, including people who had lived more than a hundred years before now.

They soon learned how to put their bodies into cruise control, so that they could lie back and relax while talking to others around them. When the sun came up in the morning, there appeared to be thousands (if not millions) of others, also dressed completely in white, all flying so high, that, from the ground, it looked like nearly parallel wispy white clouds stretching across the sky, and all moving toward a single destination.. toward an unbelievable sunrise in the East. They knew now what was ahppening. They were being pulled in the direction of the Source of Life itself. Out there in the distance, they were going to meet Josephat's God... the One who had become their Friend too.

"We're going to know soon, aren't we?" Rosy asked, as she steered her body over closer to Josephat.

"Know what?" the man asked.

"We're going to know if Moses made it."

"Ay, that we are," said Josephat with a smile. "That we are."

If you want to read more about this great event, and other incidents from this same period of time, write and ask for copies of our other two books:
"Survivors" and "Listening".

friendslearningresources@gmail.com
Friends Learning Resources
P.O. Box 8648,
Nairobi, 00200, Kenya

Swahili words

baba (_bah_-bah) father.

boda-boda (_boh_-duh-boh-duh) bicycle used as a taxi; worker who drives one of these bicycles.

chang'aa (_chahn_-gah) home brewed alcoholic drink, made from molasses.

chapati (_chuh_-_pah_-tee) flat baked piece of bread.

jambo (_jahm_-boh) hello.

jembe (_jem_-bay) short-handled, heavy hoe.

kinyosi (_kin_-_yoh_-see) beauty parlor.

matatu (_muh_-_tah_-too) van, pick-up truck, or small bus used as a taxi for many people.

matumbo (_mah_-_toom_-boh) intestines.

ni lazima (_nee luh_-_zeem_-uh) being necessary

panga (_pahn_-guh) machete.

sukuma wiki (_soo_-_koom_-uh _wik_-ee) green, leafy vegetable also known as collards or kale.

sana (_sah_-nuh) (as in 'Jambo sana') very; very much.

sawa (_sah_-wuh) okay.

shamba (_shahm_-buh) family plot of land for farming.

ugali (_oo_-_gah_-lee) moist, solid polenta made entirely of maize flour and water.

Thanks

We wish to give special thanks and
recognition to our daughter, Christine,
for the outstanding assistance that she
has given to us in writing this book.

Christine proofread the manuscript,
and offered invaluable technical advice,
based on her experiences in Kenya.

Thank you, Christine, for that and
for so much more.

--Dave & Cherry McKay

BANKING TECHNOLOGY IN KENYA

Kenya and some other African countries have been chosen for an international experiment, that is, to see if the general population will accept a new form of monetary transaction, called mobile money. This is most commonly referred to as m-pesa, although there are other forms coming out from other phone companies, such as zap, obopay, and orange money. Nokia is in the process of setting up a system for all their phones to become mobile money machines.

Please think about that as you read this book. And think about this passage of scripture from The Revelation:

"He [the Antichrist] causes all, both small and great, rich and poor, free and bond, to receive a mark in their right hand or in their foreheads: and that no man might buy or sell, save he that had the mark." Revelation 13:16 -17a

Mobile money is not the ultimate fulfillment of this prophecy, but it is an important step along the way. Another company, Verichip, is producing a tiny implant that can be used in conjunction with mobile scanners to complete the move to a cashless society. It is only a matter of time before all of this technology comes together.

We expect that there could be some very powerful moves to discredit and attack this book for what it has to say to Christians around the world, but the warning is eternally significant.

"If any man worship the beast and his image, and receive his mark in his forehead or in his hand, the same shall drink of the wine of the wrath of God... and he shall be tormented with fire and brimstone in the presence of the holy angels and in the presence of the Lamb: And the smoke of their torment ascends up forever and ever; And they have no rest day or night, who worship the beast and his image, and whosoever receives the mark of his name." Revelation 14:9-11